INTO A WATERY GRAVE . . .

"Right away, I went into the water with a bunch of other people."

"Did Kirk dive in?"

"Yeah. When Jane didn't come up after a few seconds, he didn't even wait to take off his shirt. He was frantic to find her. We all were."

"Go on."

Alice gestured helplessly. "It was awful. We kept looking and there was nothing. You know, even when people drown, they usually float to the surface. We didn't know what to do. Finally my dad had me get into my scuba equipment and go to the bottom."

"Did you see any sign of Jane's equipment down there?"

"No, nothing. But at that depth, I didn't make a real thorough check."

"Why not?"

Alice's lip quivered. "If I found her on the floor, I knew I'd just be finding her body. . . ."

Books by Christopher Pike

FALL INTO DARKNESS
FINAL FRIENDS #1: The Party
FINAL FRIENDS #2: The Dance
FINAL FRIENDS #3: The Graduation
GIMME A KISS
LAST ACT
REMEMBER ME
SCAVENGER HUNT
SPELLBOUND

Available from ARCHWAY Paperbacks

Gimme a Kiss

Christopher Pike

AN ARCHWAY PAPERBACK
Published by POCKET BOOKS

New York   London   Toronto   Sydney   Tokyo   Singapore

AN ARCHWAY PAPERBACK *Original*

An Archway Paperback published by
POCKET BOOKS, a division of Simon & Schuster Inc
1230 Avenue of the Americas, New York, NY 10020

ISBN: 0-671-68807-3

First Archway Paperback printing July 1988

15 14 13 12 11 10 9 8 7 6

AN ARCHWAY PAPERBACK and colophon are
registered trademarks of Simon & Schuster Inc.

Printed in the U.S.A.

IL 8+

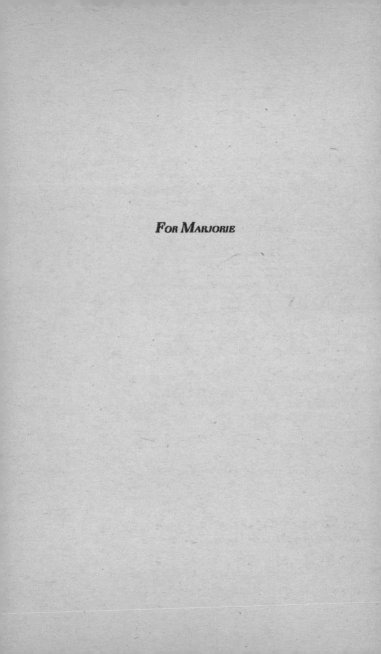

FOR MARJORIE

— PROLOGUE —

In the Room

THE GIRL LOOKED SCARED. SEATED AT THE GRAY UTILITARI-an police station table, her pale, pretty face streaked with tear tracks, she looked just like a teenager who had seen friends die.

But how many friends? Lieutenant Fisher wondered, studying Alice Palmer through the slightly ajar door as she nervously tapped the tabletop with the knuckles of her right hand, her weary eyes focused on the featureless green wall, her shapely red mouth closed, silent. It was one in the morning and the night was still young; they were still counting up the missing. Sighing, as much from fatigue as from distress over the recent tragedies—the phone had snapped him from deep sleep less than an hour ago—he pushed the door open all the way and entered the sparsely furnished interrogation room.

"Who are you?" a grossly overweight gentleman instantly demanded, lumbering to his feet on the other side of the table from Alice Palmer. Lieutenant Fisher knew who the man was without asking—the father, obviously, there to be sure his daughter's constitutional rights were not violated. And Fisher had seen his face before, in local ads, above slogans

1

reminding people that their smiles weren't a God-given right but a privilege that had to be earned with regular dental care. Dr. Palmer was one of Santa Barbara's most successful dentists.

Fisher knew he had to get the father out of the room. Otherwise, he'd never get the full story from the girl.

"I'm Lieutenant Fisher," he said, offering his hand. The dentist took it after a brief hesitation. "I've been placed in charge of this case."

Dr. Palmer looked doubtful. "Aren't you sort of young?"

Fisher had heard that question often. Oddly enough, he did not deserve the question, not exactly; he thought he looked all of his thirty-three years. The problem was, he'd been told he didn't look like a cop. His girlfriend said it was because he was too cute. Six feet tall with dark brown hair and hazel eyes, Fisher occasionally wondered what a *real* cop would look like. But he suspected his captain had called *him* in—and not another detective—for this very reason. A young lady like Alice Palmer, the captain had probably reasoned, would feel more comfortable in front of a charming face. Whatever the captain's reason, Fisher was glad he'd gotten the assignment. He was good at his job, probably the best in the department. If Alice Palmer was hiding anything, he was confident it wouldn't remain hidden.

"I've been a police officer for a dozen years." He continued, before Alice's father could respond, "May I speak to your daughter alone?"

Dr. Palmer's doubtful expression deepened. Glancing down at Alice, who appeared to welcome the request for her father to leave, he replied, "No, I want to stay."

"I'd advise against it," Fisher said firmly.

Dr. Palmer shifted nervously, putting a hand on his large belly, again glancing at his daughter. "Why? She came down here voluntarily. She isn't under arrest or anything. You can't—"

"Of course Alice isn't under arrest," Fisher interrupted smoothly. "But at least two kids have died today. A third is missing. We have to get to the bottom of this, and quickly." He paused, softening his tone. "I'd appreciate your cooperation, Dr. Palmer."

"I don't know."

"Father," Alice said, reaching across the table and putting her hand on his arm, "I'll be fine."

Dr. Palmer frowned. "You shouldn't even be here." He checked his watch. "You should be home in bed like a good girl."

Like a good girl? Fisher wondered. Given the circumstances—in the last few hours two of Alice's supposedly closest friends had been wiped off the face of the earth—it was pretty weird to be talking about being in bed and being good.

Alice started to speak, then bowed her head; it was obvious she didn't often tell her father what to do. Fisher could feel the opportunity slipping away.

"I have three sets of grieving parents waiting for me to tell them what Alice knows," he said quickly. In reality, he had only two sets of parents—they had not been able to locate Jane Retton's mother and father— and neither of them even knew he was trying to question Alice. Yet the lie caused him no guilt. He could see Dr. Palmer start to waver as he walked around the table to stand behind Alice.

3

"I won't have you harassing my angel," he said, putting his fat hands on his daughter's shoulders. "I won't stand for it."

Fisher nodded. "I'm just here to listen."

The father pointed to the door. "I'm going to be right outside in the hallway, young man. I'm only giving you a few minutes."

"Fine." Fisher intended to keep her all night, if that was what it took. He had already alerted another officer to hustle Dr. Palmer off to the snack bar the instant he had the dentist out of the room.

Dr. Palmer spoke to his daughter. "You call me if you need me. You hear?"

Alice smiled weakly, nodding. Fisher stepped aside and let Dr. Palmer by. As he shut the dentist out, Fisher wished there were a lock on the door.

Now we begin, he thought, turning to Alice. It was only then that he began to fully appreciate what an attractive young woman she was. Her shiny black hair hung long and straight over her shoulders, but fell in large, soft waves close to her round cheeks. There was an innocence in her features, in the smoothness of her skin and the wideness of her gray eyes that the anxiety of the situation had not erased. The father's nickname echoed in Fisher's head.

Angel Alice.

Yet as Fisher sat down across from her, he noticed her left hand had moved to the corner of her mouth, as though she were subconsciously afraid of what might pass her lips. Or perhaps she was just trying to hide a sore that appeared to be forming there. He knew from experience he could read too much meaning into body language. Signs of stress did not necessarily imply guilt.

4

He opened the book he had been holding, Wilcox High's annual from the year before. He placed it at such an angle that both Alice and he would be able to look at it. The dead or missing teenagers, he had been told, were all pictured in the junior class section.

"Your father watches out for you, doesn't he?" he remarked, carefully searching the pages for the last names he had memorized a few minutes before.

"He's always been that way. It wasn't you."

Fisher smiled. "I bet he's hard on your boyfriends when they come to visit."

"Sometimes."

He nodded toward a diet root beer standing beside her on the table, searching for anything to break the ice before getting down to business. "Does that have NutraSweet in it?"

"I think so, yeah."

"Being the daughter of a dentist, I bet there isn't a lot of sugar in your house?"

"No, not much. Except at holidays and stuff."

He smiled again. "Tell me the truth: when you're out with friends, what do you order?"

"Pardon?"

"I bet you never ask for a diet anything. I had a girlfriend in college whose dad was a dentist. Once she got out of the house, she turned into an instant sugar freak. I'd take her out to dinner and she'd have three kinds of dessert, nothing else. But she flossed all the time. I guess some habits die hard. Before I'd kiss her good night, she'd pull out those damn plastic strings."

Alice's hand slipped a notch from her mouth, and she allowed a trace of a smile. "Sounds like me. I think I'm the only one in school who has floss in her gym locker."

"I'm not surprised. Hey, want a Coke? A real Coke?"

She hesitated. "My dad—"

"I'm going to have one."

"Yeah, sure. All right."

There was a soft drink machine in the corner. He had plenty of quarters. A minute later they were both sipping sodas. He had lied about his college girlfriend in an effort to give them something in common. And he wanted her drinking a Coke with him so they'd be sharing something the father would disapprove of; a little thing, but such a psychological ploy could often mean the difference between hearing the truth and being told lies. He went back to the yearbook, with Alice now following his search through the pages.

"Alice, before we go into what happened, there're some people I'd like you to give me a brief description of. Okay?"

"Sure."

He came to the first one: Patty Brane. Naturally, Fisher recognized her; they had met not more than ten minutes before. She was currently waiting in a nearby room with her parents and a three-piece-suited lawyer who had told her not to breathe a word about anything.

Like Alice, Patty was pretty, though her attractiveness was of different sort. Patty had obviously been around. In the short time Fisher had been in the room with her, she had checked out his body from head to tail. And her own body was nothing to laugh at; these kids seemed to be developing quicker each year.

"You know her?" Fisher asked, pointing to the picture. Patty's blond hair had been a lot shorter and a lot darker the year before.

Alice nodded. "Patty, yeah."

"Is she a friend of yours?"

"No. I mean, we don't talk much."

"Did you know she's here at the station?"

"No."

"What's she like?"

"What do you mean?"

"Is she nice? Is she mean? Is she smart?"

Alice thought for a moment. "I don't like saying bad things about people."

"You two don't get along?"

"Well, not really. We don't hang out with the same people. But . . ."

"Yes?"

Alice paused. "What did she say about me?"

He didn't want Alice to know exactly what he knew, which was next to nothing. "Not much. But as you were saying?"

Alice averted her eyes. "She's bad."

"Bad?"

"She's loose, you know, with guys."

"I see." He turned a couple of pages, coming to Kirk Donner. Blond and tan, Kirk had the same surf-and-sand look as Patty; however, he wasn't nearly as attractive. There was a cockiness in the line of his mouth, and his curly hair needed combing. But the photo included enough of his wide shoulders to make it clear Kirk Donner wasn't a kid it would have been easy to mess with; he had a build.

"How about this guy?" he asked.

Alice winced. "That's Kirk. He was Jane's boy-friend."

"And Jane was your best friend?"

"Yes."

"Did you like Kirk?"

The question hurt. Her hand went back to her mouth. "I used to like him a lot."

"What happened?"

"He was—he used to be my boyfriend."

"Did you break up with him or did he break up with you?"

The question was awfully blunt, but she didn't hesitate to answer. "I left him."

"Why?"

"We—didn't get along."

"Did Jane and he get along?"

Alice took a breath. "They seemed to."

Fisher closed the annual over his forearm. "Are you okay?"

She nodded. "I'm fine."

He reopened the book, turned more pages. Sharon Less was next. Although she was plain compared to Alice and Patty, her smile literally jumped off the page. Fisher suspected she was the friendliest of the lot.

"Tell me about Sharon," he said.

"She's my friend. I mean, the three of us, Jane and Sharon and I hang out together." Alice paused. "She's nice."

She had not spoken of Sharon in the past tense. "Do you know where she is now?"

"No."

"You're sure?"

"I thought—"

"What?"

"I don't know. I don't know where she is."

Fisher let the moment hang, finally asking, "Is it possible she's dead?"

Alice appeared genuinely confused. "Don't you know, one way or the other?"

"No. As the captain must have told you, we can't locate her."

A tear rolled down her cheek, and she lowered her head. "Maybe she'll show up."

"I hope so."

They were interrupted by a knock on the door. "Yes?" Fisher called, hoping it wasn't Alice's father. His wish was granted. Young and eager, Officer Rick pushed open the door and stuck his head inside. Rick was actually his first name; he looked too wet behind the ears to be addressed by his last name, which was Kraken.

"Dr. Hilt wants you to know he's doing the positive I.D. on the body now," Rick said. "He told me it wouldn't take long."

Fisher stood quickly and ushered Rick back into the hallway outside the door. He wanted Alice to hear only what he decided she should hear. "I thought he didn't have much to work with?"

"He has the skull intact."

"Does he know yet if the remains are female or male?"

"Hilt didn't say one way or the other." Officer Rick shook his head, paling. "I helped bring in what he does have. What a mess. It gives me the creeps."

Fisher searched the deserted hallway. "Where's Dr. Palmer?"

"The captain's entertaining him in the snack bar."

"Good. Keep him there. And keep me up to date."

Fisher returned to the room, sat down, and again flipped through the annual, searching for one last picture.

9

"Alice," he said casually, "what am I investigating here?"

She wiped at her face with the sleeve of her light blue sweater. "I don't understand?"

"It's late, Alice. I was told you woke up your dad and had him bring you down to the station because you knew something about these deaths that the rest of us don't?"

Alice nodded. "I do."

"How did you know we had another death tonight?"

"I heard about it on the news. On the radio."

Fisher silently cursed the local media. "Which station?"

"I don't remember."

He paused in his search through the book, stared her straight in the eye. "Was either Kirk or Sharon or Jane murdered?"

"No." She considered the question for a moment. "Kirk's death was accidental. Though, in a way, it was Jane's fault. And I think—I think Jane killed herself."

Fisher turned another page. "The coroner is examining what is left of the body we found up in the hills. Are you saying he will identify the remains as belonging to Jane?"

"Yes. Did your people only find one body up in the hills?"

"So far. Will we find another?"

She shrugged stiffly. "I was just wondering, that's all."

He had reached the *R*s. Jane Retton's photograph was in the top right corner of the page. She had an interesting face. There was none of the frivolousness he had glimpsed in the others. Staring at her blue eyes, set deep beneath her shiny brown bangs, he wondered why she had chosen not to smile for the camera. Although she did not possess the obvious beauty of Alice and Patty, there was something alluring in the way she held her head; she seemed to be keeping herself apart from her surroundings. And yet, at the same time, she looked somehow very vulnerable.

And I'll never meet her, Fisher thought. The day's losses suddenly hit him in a personal way. A few months before graduating from high school was a turning point in a kid's life. Something in Jane's face caused him to believe she could have done great things had she been given the chance.

"She never liked having her picture taken," Alice said, watching him.

"Why was that?"

"She never thought she looked like the person they had photographed."

Fisher sighed silently, closed the book. "Tell me more."

"She was intense."

Interesting choice of words. Fisher would have said Alice herself was intense. He reached for the legal notepad that lay on the table, then pulled out his pen. Leaving several lines after each name, he jotted down the principal characters they would be discussing, adding a brief notation to aid him in keeping them straight.

Patty: Sexy bad girl. Disliked by Alice. Refuses to talk.

Kirk: Boyfriend of Jane and Alice. May have died accidentally.

Sharon: Friend of Jane and Alice. Big smile. Missing.

Jane: Friend of Alice and Sharon. Intense. Possible suicide.

Fisher leaned back in his chair, reached for his Coke. He would keep his notes on Alice in his head. "Tell me what happened," he said.

Alice swallowed. "I don't know where to start."

"At the beginning."

Alice closed her eyes for a moment. "That would be yesterday morning, or rather Friday morning—I guess it's already Sunday morning now. Yeah, that's when things got all messed up. Jane started it with what she wrote in her diary."

"You know what she wrote?"

"Yes. A fantasy."

— CHAPTER 1 —

THE DIARY WAS NOT A REAL DIARY, BUT AN ORDINARY three-hundred-page spiral notebook, with numerous ink doodles on its yellow covers. Later, Jane Retton was to realize that if she'd had a real diary, her life would not have taken the awful turn it did on that fourth Friday of her senior year.

The notebook was an old friend; she had written in it weekly since her sophomore year. Because her handwriting was small and precise, she still had a good fifty blank pages left. She stuck with it, instead of purchasing a more fashionable model, because she seldom had a spare penny to her name, and because no one would ever mistake the notebook for a diary, so no one would be tempted to take a peek inside. The latter reason was the main one, and yet it had occurred to her from time to time that the use of reverse psychology might very well turn against her someday. Jane Retton did not suffer from excessive paranoia, but she did like to be careful.

That particular Friday morning had started early for her. Her mom and dad were going camping in the Sierras for a long weekend, and she had gotten up at dawn to help them make sandwiches and load the car. Although they were leaving without her, she shared in

13

their excitement at getting away; she would be embarking on her own trip the following day. Along with about sixty of her classmates, she would sail to the Santa Barbara Islands to swim and hike and goof off. She had been looking forward to the trip for a long time.

Once her parents had left, Jane waited for her friends, Alice Palmer and Sharon Less, to pick her up for school. Despite her meager resources, Jane had bought a car of her own, a green '78 Toyota Corolla. She had saved for it with the salary she earned working part-time in Alice's dad's dental office. Unfortunately, the carburetor had clogged arteries or something and wasn't burning gasoline in a steady stream; the car kept stalling. Next paycheck she would have someone look at it, but until then, she didn't mind using Alice Palmer as a chauffeur. Dentists made out all right, and Dr. Palmer couldn't spend enough on his "little girl." Alice owned a Jaguar.

It was Dr. Palmer who had rented the sailboat and crew for the weekend excursion to the islands. Indeed, he was to be their skipper. Jane had sailed with him before. He knew how to handle himself on the water.

While waiting for her ride, Jane decided to write for a bit in her diary, and retreated to the desk in her bedroom. The desk faced a spacious north window, granting her, day in and day out, a view of Santa Barbara's hills—another place she enjoyed visiting. Sharon's parents owned a cabin in those hills.

Jane slipped her diary-notebook from its hiding place at the bottom of the left-hand drawer. She didn't need time to decide what she was going to write about; she had been daydreaming about it for a while now, ever since she had gone out with her boyfriend last

Saturday. She was going to put down on paper what it had been like to make love to Kirk Donner.

But before she recorded the passionate night for a posterity she had no intention of ever letting see—never mind read—her diary, she turned to the page on which she had described how Kirk first asked her out.

August 8th (30 days of vacation left and counting)

Dear Diary,

It happened! I knew it would! Kirk asked me out on a date. I can hardly believe it. I'm so excited. I'm practically talking to myself. I've just got to tell you about it.

I was getting ice cream at the Häagen-Dazs in the mall. I was standing there trying to figure out what I wanted when suddenly I had an urge for a banana split. Now, you know as well as I do (since we are the same person) that I have never had a banana split in my life. I don't even like bananas. The way things turned out, my urge to eat a split must have come from somewhere "out there." Coincidence can't explain it. You'll see what I mean.

Anyway, so I told the girl what I wanted, and she dug around and came up with what turned out to be the only banana they had left. It was a real whopper. It was so big that I was sure—to make up the difference in cost and stuff—they would hardly give me any ice cream. I actually started wondering what I had gotten myself into.

Then Kirk walked in. At first he didn't even see me. He went right up to the girl behind the counter and said he wanted a banana split. Of course the girl immediately pointed to me and said I had taken the last banana. Kirk smiled when he saw it was me.

"Then make it one big split and we'll share it," he told the girl.

Now, I admit it was sort of macho of him to assume I wanted to share my split with him. What was even stranger, though, was that the chick working there didn't even ask if that was okay with me. She went ahead and scooped out the ice cream and let Kirk decide what toppings we were to have. I didn't care. Kirk must have just come from the beach. There was sand in his hair and his arms were tanned darker than usual. He looked great. Plus he paid for the split.

We sat in the center of the mall, next to the fountain. I don't really remember what we talked about. The way his blue eyes stayed focused on me the whole time was distracting. But he did say Alice and he weren't even speaking to each other anymore. Listening, I received the distinct impression that that was fine with him. I wondered if Alice hadn't been exaggerating when she told me he was taking their breakup hard. Still, after all the two of them had gone through together, I felt kind of guilty eating out of the same dish with Kirk. But not nearly as guilty as I did when he asked me if I was doing anything on Friday.

I'll tell you why I said I was free. First, I *was* free. Sure, Sharon had talked about us going to a movie, but Sharon and I have been going to movies together since we were allowed to go around the block. I knew Sharon would understand. Then there was the fact that Alice, who knows I've always liked Kirk, has told me more than once—twice, I think—that she couldn't care less if I dated her old boyfriend. I know, I know—what she says and what she means are not necessarily the same thing. Like I said, the guilt was there.

But he is sooo cute! How could I say no?

When I went to write down my address for him, he told me he already knew where I lived. How about that? I think this is the beginning of a romance that has been a long time in the planning. Since he asked me out, I've had two more banana splits and I've loved them both.

Jane smiled as she read the last line. It was a smile that stayed with her as she picked up her pen, turned to the first blank page, and started to describe the culmination of that shared ice cream in the mall.

October 6th (138 days of high school left and counting)
Dear Diary,

I've been very naughty. I've gone and done what no good girl should do. I've lost my virginity. And I know exactly where I lost it. But let me tell you, there's no getting it back.

Last Saturday was the big day. We started things off at the beach. The sun couldn't have been brighter. The water felt like ice. Because I hadn't planned on going in, I had on my French bikini. But I went in anyway, and Kirk couldn't take his eyes off me. Almost lost the blasted thing a couple of times.

We ate, took a walk in the park, went to a movie—purely inconsequential activities compared to what happened next. When Kirk finally took me home, we discovered my parents were out. I asked if he'd like to come in for tea. I don't know, maybe he likes tea. I never got to make it for him.

The house was pitch-black when we entered. I must admit, I made the first move. As Kirk reached for the light, his arm accidentally brushed my side, and I took his hands and touched the knuckles to my lips. He couldn't even see me

"Gimme a kiss," I whispered.

Jane paused to reflect, not on what she was going to say, but on how she was going to say it. One's first sexual experience—it was something that had to be handled delicately. It was crucial she get the wording just the way she wanted it. Thoughts were powerful—transformed into words, they practically turned into reality.

Kirk and Jane hadn't really made love.

In fact, they had never even shared a banana split.

She might have been the only girl in California who lied to her diary more often than she lied to her mother. She was wise enough to know that by doing so she was moving perilously close to lying to herself. But, what the hell, her life wasn't that great, and it wasn't against the law to pretend.

Kirk had asked her out for the first time over ice cream, and it had happened at the mall, but otherwise, she had made up the scenario. More importantly, she had altered its tone. When Kirk had entered the Häagen-Dazs store, she had gotten so nervous her stomach had twisted into one huge knot. She had always liked him—at least, she had always liked the way he looked—even before Alice realized he was alive. He hadn't ordered for her, and probably the only reason they had started talking was because he had been nineteen cents short when he went to pay for his shake; she'd had to help him out. After that, he'd undoubtedly felt obligated to show her a little attention. They had sat and chatted on a bench next to the noisy arcade. (There was no fountain in the mall, but her diary didn't know any better.) And when he finally did pop the magical question, she had hardly recognized it for what it was. He'd asked if he could stop by on Sunday. Seemed his TV wasn't working and there was a baseball game he'd made a bet with a buddy about. Sure, she'd said.

She hadn't thought of Alice or felt guilty. There hadn't seemed much reason to, not on day one.

But if their beginning was less than romantic, it *was* a beginning. They were still going out together, not every week, but almost. He wasn't going out with anyone else. And, although they were two different types, they got along well. Kirk was, in his own words, a perpetual goof-off. He had too much energy. Sitting still in class was torture for him. Yet school athletics had never caught his imagination; too many coaches to listen to, she supposed. He loved nothing better than to buy a pizza and a six-pack—he could easily pass for twenty-one with his hefty build—and toss a Frisbee on the beach for hours, eating when he got hungry, swimming when he got hot. He would be graduating with their class, but no one would ask him to speak before they handed out the diplomas.

Jane, on the other hand, qualified as something of a book person. Her grades weren't outstanding, and no one—God forbid—would have called her a nerd. Yet reading and writing meant a lot to her. Indeed, Alice had accused her of living in a fantasy world, and it was true she enjoyed tales of fairies and dragons. Lately, however, love stories had become her staple, both teen and adult ones. Going out with Kirk probably had a lot to do with that. She had never had a boyfriend before. She was determined to hold on to him.

The passionate side of the relationship didn't exist entirely in her head. Last Saturday, as Kirk had walked her to the front door, she *had* said, "Gimme a kiss." And he had kissed her, long and deep. The event had taken place in space and time. What did it matter if he hadn't really spent the night?

I'll have to spend a long time on how we undressed each other, she thought, chewing on her pen, pondering over her diary. *Buttons and zippers are every bit as important as anatomical parts.*

But Jane wasn't given a chance to satisfy Kirk or herself. A life-and-death situation suddenly broke out in her backyard. Her cute white rabbit, Easter, was being attacked by a neighboring cat.

"Get! Get!" she screamed, leaping to her feet and flipping her chair over. The instant the cat entered the yard, Easter had wisely dashed behind a corner cactus. The cat had hesitated at the sight of the prickly thorns and had paused to listen to Jane's screams. But she had had a bunny when she was ten that had lost its throat to a bloodthirsty Persian. Cats were nice cuddly animals until they crossed something weak that they could eat. This cat wasn't going to leave unless kicked out. Turning, Jane raced for the back door.

As she burst into the yard a moment later, her heart skipped in her chest. In the seconds the drama had been out of her sight, the cat had chased the rabbit from behind the cactus and tackled it by its hind legs in the middle of the grass. Poor Easter, his whiskers twitching horribly, couldn't even cry out.

"Stop!" Jane shouted. "Dammit, stop!"

The cat wasn't listening. It's claws grappled over Easter's back, twisting the bunny's neck closer to its mouth. Jane realized she didn't have time to cross the forty feet that separated them. Fortunately, her mother used hundreds of smooth black pebbles to provide an attractive base for the yard's bushes; there were dozens of them at her feet. Grabbing one, she pitched it at the cat as hard as she could.

Her aim couldn't have been better. Rock contacted skull. The cat hissed and let go of Easter. Before Jane could reach for another rock, the monster had vaulted the fence and disappeared to nurse its headache. Jane ran toward Easter, picked up her quivering bunny, and cuddled him in her arms.

"It's all right. Kitty's gone. Shh, don't be scared. There, everything is better now. You didn't get eaten."

Jane knew as well as the next person that rabbits were about as dumb as the lettuce they nibbled on. Nevertheless, she kept up her mushy reassurances for a few minutes, and Easter did seem to understand enough to stop shaking. There were a couple of bright red spots on his snow-white fur, but Jane could find no visible cuts, and the bleeding seemed to have stopped at these two drops. Putting him back in his wire cage, she said, "You seem to have only two choices, Easter. To run free and die young or to stay a prisoner and grow fat and old."

Despite the lightness of her remarks, she continued to tremble herself. Blood, even in small amounts, made her very uncomfortable.

She was walking slowly back into the house when she heard a car pulling into the driveway. Her friends were early. Before she could reach the front door, Sharon burst inside.

"Hi, Jane, how are you doing? You look great. What's new? Got anything to eat? I'm starving."

"I'm fine. Thanks for the compliment. You look great, too. No, nothing's new, but there's food in the refrigerator."

"Super." Sharon swept by her, skinny as a bean pole. Sharon could eat whatever she wanted and never gain a pound. Nothing like a hyperactive thyroid to keep off the inches. She made even Kirk look like someone on tranquilizers. Jane supposed that she and Sharon had remained friends so long—since kindergarten—because they balanced each other. No matter how slow she might feel on a particular morning, Sharon always got her going.

"Doughnuts, you've got doughnuts. Perfect," Sharon said. She grabbed the box and a carton of milk from the fridge and hurried over to the table. A brunette like herself, Sharon had recently taken to wearing her hair punk-short. The change had been a bad move—at least in Jane's opinion. Without her long curls, Sharon could easily be mistaken for an undernourished guy. Yet Jane also had to admire the carelessness with which Sharon had thrown away years of hair growing. Sharon honestly didn't care about her appearance.

"Is that all you're having for breakfast?" Jane asked.

"This doughnut?" Sharon mumbled, her mouth full. "No."

"Good."

"No, I was thinking of having *two* doughnuts. If that's okay with you? There was nothing in our house except bran cereal and brown rice. My mom's on a real health kick. Where's your mom, anyway?"

"My parents have gone to the mountains for the weekend." Jane glanced out the window. "Why hasn't Alice come in?"

Sharon took a swig of milk from the carton. "She brought you that wet suit you wanted. I think she's brushing the sand off it or something."

Last year, Alice and Jane had been in a pottery class together. Jane had known Alice slightly ever since they'd entered high school, but it was only when they shared the same messy clay-covered table that they had started to become friends. After a few weeks of talking, Alice had invited her for a spin on her dad's boat. The cruise had started Jane off on what turned out to be her most treasured hobby—scuba diving. Alice had been diving since childhood, and Jane wasted no time signing up for a local YMCA course after listening to Alice's descriptions of what it was like to patrol the ocean's floor. Floating weightless with immeasurable leagues of black water beneath her and a hundred feet of sun-streaked blue above always made Jane feel as though she had entered the space of the alien solar systems found so often in the books she read.

Scuba diving wasn't cheap. If Alice's dad hadn't thrown in all the free compressed air she wanted as partial compensation for her work at his dental office, she probably would have had to abandon the sport at the beginning. As it was, she could now handle herself under water almost as well as on land.

"Maybe I should go and help her," Jane said.

Sharon shrugged. "She'll be here in a moment. Sit down, have a doughnut with me."

"I don't want one."

"Go ahead, or I'll finish the box."

Jane sat down. She actually loved doughnuts and always wanted one. "What time are we setting out for the islands tomorrow?" she asked, biting into a French curl.

"Alice says at the crack of dawn. Her dad's going to leave then, no matter who's late. Oh, I told her you wanted Kirk to come. She said she didn't care."

"Sharon! I told you I'd ask her myself."

"Yeah, but you wouldn't have. You were afraid to. I did you the favor."

Jane glanced again out the window, lowering her voice. "How did she take it?"

"I just told you."

"But how did she say it? Did she look surprised or what?"

"She bit her lip and screamed through soul-rending sobs that she didn't care. I don't know! I really don't think she cares. Don't worry about it. I'm not."

"Of course you're not. He's not your boyfriend."

Sharon smiled slyly. "Didn't you once tell me that what was yours was mine?"

"I never said that."

"Yes, you did. Remember when we were in kindergarten and I wanted to use your crayons?"

"Oh, well, in that case, I'll share a sleeping bag with

Kirk one night, and you can have him the next. Sound fair?"

"I'll go along with that."

Sharon was always joking about getting Kirk for herself. Lately, it had begun to annoy Jane. She changed the subject. "Find out when the judge will let you have your license back?"

Sharon had received one too many tickets. She had this bad habit of stopping at red lights, looking both ways, and going if the coast appeared clear. Her dad had bought her a ten-speed bike to get around while her license was suspended. She often rode it to school.

"No, and it pisses me off. The judge says I can start driving again as soon as I demonstrate I can handle a vehicle in a responsible fashion. Now, I ask you, how can I do that when I'm not allowed behind the wheel?"

"Maybe he's going to evaluate you by how many snails you run over on your Schwinn."

"Wouldn't surprise me one bit." Sharon stood suddenly. "I've got to go to the bathroom."

"Don't use my parents'. My mom cleaned it spotless before she left."

Sharon nodded, taking an extra doughnut with her. "I'll use the one in your room."

Alice appeared, carrying a scraggly wet suit, a couple of minutes after Sharon left. Alice had already given Jane a suit—she had in fact permanently lent Jane all the equipment necessary to scuba dive—but this suit, though old and torn, had full legs, and would be warmer. A cousin or somebody had mailed it to Alice.

"There's a rip along the right shoulder," Alice said

as Jane let her into the house. "I put some thread in the car trunk so you could sew it up, but now I can't find it."

Jane smiled, taking the wet suit and holding it out in front of her. "Thanks. This will keep me toasty warm, no matter how deep I go. Don't worry about the tear. My mom has thread."

Alice took a seat beside the half-finished box of doughnuts, her long black hair skimming the table, beautiful in contrast to her white skin. Alice spent a lot of time outdoors but never seemed to tan. Sharon often referred to her as a vampire. Jane suspected she used special creams to protect herself from premature wrinkles.

"The thread I had was from the sporting goods store," Alice said. "Salt water couldn't damage it. But I guess ordinary thread will do for this weekend."

"Sharon says we have to be up early."

Alice nodded, her big gray eyes serious, as always. "Better not stay out late tonight."

"I don't have anything planned," she lied. She had intended to go bowling with Kirk. Well, maybe they could go early and still be in bed at a respectable hour. "Hungry?"

Alice frowned at the doughnuts. "I shouldn't."

"Go ahead, before Sharon eats the whole box."

Alice was easy to convince. And Jane helped herself to another, figuring she could burn off the extra calories with an extra long swim the next day.

She probably wouldn't have offered Alice the doughnuts if she'd remembered that Alice would want to brush her teeth afterward. Since Sharon had not reappeared, they ended up in her parents' bathroom. Alice carried a toothbrush in her purse, plus a small tube of Crest. Because Alice was being so hygienically conscious, Jane felt she had to join in. They ended up talking through mouthfuls of foam, mostly about nothing. As they were finishing, Jane noticed Alice was developing a cold sore. It hadn't been there last week.

"Want some Blistex for that?" Jane offered, opening the medicine cabinet.

"For what?"

"Your mouth. It's good stuff."

Alice was putting away her things, her head down. "No, thank you."

"You might want it tomorrow. The sun can make those things worse."

Alice found a comb, began to fix her hair. "That's all right."

Jane closed the medicine cabinet. "What's the name of the sailboat your dad's rented?"

Alice brightened. "*Wild Wind.* It's gorgeous; I wish we owned it. From bow to stern, it's ninety feet. I was thinking maybe we could invite a few more people."

Jane smiled. "Sixty's not enough for you?"

"I know, it looks like I'm trying to win a popularity contest. But I really do feel sorry for all the people in our class who won't be able to come."

Jane recognized the sentiment as genuine. Alice's conscience pricked easily. "You've invited as many as you can. Nobody's going to hold a grudge against you."

Alice sighed. "I hope you're right. Oh, Sharon told me about Kirk. Tell him he's welcome to come."

"Sure it won't bother you having him there?"

"I'm sure."

"Are you positive?"

Alice hesitated. "Yeah." Then she smiled. "Besides, I've got to make it up to you somehow."

"Make what up to me?"

"I've invited Patty Brane."

"What? Why?" Patty Brane was head cheerleader. Jane had inadvertently offended her—and all of Wilcox High's cheerleaders, for that matter—in an article she had written for the school paper. Since then, Patty had been verbally hassling her whenever it was convenient. As they shared the same homeroom, that was every morning.

"Patty's dad goes to the same church we do. My dad said I had to put her on my list. Don't worry, it's a big boat. If you're lucky, you won't even have to talk to her."

"If I'm lucky, she won't push me overboard." Jane rinsed off her toothbrush, muttering, "Kirk probably won't even be up when we shove off."

Alice frowned. "I told you he's perfectly welcome."

"Exes are never perfectly anything."

Alice stared at her for an instant. "They're not, are they?"

"Alice—"

"It's okay," she interrupted, shaking herself. "Come on, let's talk about something else."

"All right."

Alice checked her watch. "Where's Sharon? I wanted to get to school a bit early. There're a lot of people I have to find and remind about the early departure."

"She's in the other bathroom. She's been in there forever. I'll go get her."

Alice touched her arm. "No, I'll get her. Fix your hair. It looks like you've been in a wrestling match."

"I was, with a cat," Jane said, picking up a brush. The sudden memory of the incident filled her with an odd sense of foreboding. There seemed to be no reason for it. Surely Easter was safe in his cage. A tiger couldn't paw through that wire.

Sharon and Alice reappeared a few minutes later, Alice again mentioning the need for haste. Finishing her hair, Jane dashed into her bedroom and collected her books from her desk.

Easter will be fine, she told herself. *I'm worrying about nothing.*

Nevertheless, the disquiet followed her all the way to school.

— Chapter II —

Wilcox High was beautiful. A soft ocean breeze blew steadily through its clean redbrick wings. Between classes, no matter how great the turmoil of a particular day, Jane could always look west through the spaces between the trees and the crowds to see the wide expanse of water, and feel at ease.

Leaving the parking lot after stashing the Jaguar, Alice parted company to hunt down her prospective guests. Sharon and Jane made straight for their lockers. The day was sunny, good weather for swimming and sailing. Jane hoped it would keep up.

"Going out with Kirk tonight?" Sharon asked.

"I don't know," Jane said. "I've got to be at the clinic from three to seven. And Dr. Palmer always keeps me late. It might get too late to do anything."

"What's it like working for that walrus, anyway? Does he make you take prayer breaks or what?"

"He's not that bad. Once you learn the secret of avoiding his lectures, you don't hear them too often."

"What's the secret?"

"Always look extremely busy." Jane smiled, readjusting the shoulder strap on her book bag. Lately, she'd had so much homework and had been reading so many books that the bag had become a necessity. "And try never to speak to him."

Sharon laughed. "I don't see how Alice can stand him."

"She doesn't seem to mind."

"Yeah, brand-new cars on her birthdays make life bearable. So what about your folks? They're away for the weekend, right? Sounds like the coast is clear for you and Kirk. You're not going to let this opportunity pass, are you?"

If Sharon wasn't hungry and talking about food, she was talking about sex. If you could believe her—and she exaggerated so much and so often that she never had reason to lie—she had slept with three guys, all from the nearby University of Santa Barbara, all three unverifiable conquests. Having listened to her luridly detailed accounts, Jane figured Sharon had probably had her breasts fondled a couple of times.

"We've all got to get up early tomorrow," Jane said.

Sharon snorted. "You'll be out of the clinic by eight at the latest. You can get started by nine. Just how much time do you think a teenage boy needs, anyway?"

"I don't know." None of the books she had read on the subject had told her.

Sharon bumped her hip, switching to a confidential tone. "Don't you? Come on, Jane. We're best friends. What was he like?"

"I told you, we've never done it."

"Swear to God? I don't believe you. Come on, was it great or gross or what? I know you did it."

"How do you know?"

"I just do. If you don't tell me, I'll ask Kirk."

"Ask him."

"You're really going to keep it to yourself? Man, you're no fun. And here I tell you when I read a *Playgirl* magazine."

Just then Jane spotted Kirk. He was leaning against the science building, talking to a blonde in a red pants suit. The girl was facing the other way, and Jane was unable to identify her. As Jane watched, she patted Kirk on the shoulder and disappeared around the corner of the building.

"Sharon," she said, suddenly changing course, "I'll catch up with you later. Bye."

"Swell. Wonderful. Split when it suits you. Don't worry about me. I didn't have anything worth saying. Good-bye. Have fun. God."

Kirk was still near the building when she caught up with him. Seeing her coming, he broke into a grin. Kirk's mouth almost demanded that he smile; otherwise, wearing a relaxed expression, he looked angry. But making him laugh always came easy for Jane. She just had to tell him how neat he was. He pretended never to believe her.

"Hey, don't I know you, girl?"

She shook her head. "You must be mistaking me for another."

He scratched his unkempt blond hair. "I could swear you were that chick in that bar last night."

She moved closer, into his welcoming hug, staring up into his slightly bloodshot blue eyes. He might very well have been hitting the bottle the previous night; he often drank when he was bored.

"Must be hard remembering when there've been so many bars," she said as he wrapped his arms around her. "And so many girls."

Already, she had decided not to ask him who he had been talking to. His hugs had that effect on her; they made her feel secure.

"Ain't it the truth?" he said. "You're Ann, right?"

"No."

"Hilary?" He tugged on her hair.

"Starts with a *J*."

"Julie."

"Close. Ja—"

"Janice."

"Jane."

"I knew it." He started to kiss her.

"Wait," she said, suddenly stepping back, smiling quickly to soften the rejection. Public demonstration of affection always made her uneasy. But not Kirk; he could make out on her parents' couch with her parents sitting on it.

"That's fine," he said just as quickly. A slight awkwardness hung between them. It happened occasionally; they didn't know each other *that* well. Jane reached in her bag, pulled out a paperback.

"I got you the next Narnia Chronicle. You'll like it. There's this part— Well, I won't spoil it for you. It's really magical. You'll have to read it."

Since they had started dating, she had been trying to make literature a part of his daily diet. Initially, she had made little headway. He'd taken a dozen of her favorites and put them on his bedroom shelf and left them there. Then she had realized—to her mild horror—that he wasn't reading the books because he *couldn't*. His vocabulary simply wasn't large enough. This was more a reflection on their mediocre educational system, in her opinion, and on his nonexistent study habits than on his I.Q. He was easily as smart as ninety percent of the kids at Wilcox High (well, maybe fifty percent). Since the discovery, she had been feeding him stories she had read when she was in sixth grade. He honestly appeared to be enjoying them.

"That's a far-out-looking lion," he remarked, studying the cover.

"Wait till you see what he can do with his voice. He's got all kinds of powers."

"I'll read it. Thanks, kid." He stuffed the book—probably creasing the cover, she couldn't help noticing—into his back pocket and glanced restlessly about. "Still want me on the boat this weekend?"

"I'd be bored without you. Alice doesn't mind."

He scowled. "Believe that and you'll believe anything." He cleared his throat. "Anyway, I wasn't thinking about Alice. Her old man's the one I'm not looking forward to spending time with. That dude can't stand the sight of me."

"Why?"

He shrugged. "I don't know. Must have offended him somehow. Of course that's easy to do."

Jane lowered her head. "You don't have to go. *I* don't even have to go."

Kirk laughed. "You've been talking about it forever. Nah, let's do it. If it doesn't work out, we can always swim back to shore."

She laughed with him. "Yeah, all twenty miles."

The bell rang. He hugged her again and they made plans to have lunch together. The day was off to a good start.

Homeroom for her was in the drama studio. There were plenty of seats, and when she arrived late she usually chose one as far from Patty Brane as possible.

However, if Patty came in after Jane, she invariably sat close enough to touch her. And Patty always had a couple of buddies with her.

Jane's problem with the head cheerleader had begun two weeks earlier. Wilcox High published a bimonthly paper. Because she had done well in creative writing her junior year, the teacher who oversaw the paper, Mr. Hype—the name was fitting—had requested she write articles for *The Last Word* on a regular basis. She had agreed before she learned what he wanted her to cover. Just her luck, it turned out to be sports. At that point in her life, she had seen enough football games to know you got six points for a touchdown, a bonus one if you kicked the extra point, three points for a field goal, and another four downs if you could move the ball ten yards. She wasn't totally ignorant. But if she was going to put her name on a piece, she wanted it to be something special. Before the opening game, she cloistered herself in the library with every book she could find on the sport. In retrospect, she realized she should have spoken to a few guys on the team. On the other hand, her research might have taught her *too* much about football.

In the first game of the season, Wilcox got crushed by twenty points. When she wrote her article, Jane stated that they would continue to lose as long as they remained so predictable; the team had run on all but three plays. No one on the paper had told her she wasn't supposed to offer her own personal views on the subject. Then again, if it had been a mistake to criticize the coaching, it had been a mortal sin—judging by what followed—to remark on the cheerleaders.

She didn't believe she was a negative person. It had

just struck her as weird that the girls on the squad were busy flaunting their bodies seconds before the opposing team scored. The actual lines she used to describe this were—in her opinion—quite innocent, if not amusing.

Trak High put another six points on the board at the end of the third period on a two-yard quarterback sneak. Not to worry, Wilcox's indomitable pep squad took a two-minute hair-and-lipstick break and were smiling pretty when our boys got their hands on the ball again on the ensuing kickoff.

Mr. Hype published the article without so much as a passing comment. Funny how people couldn't recognize a controversial item until it became controversial.

When *The Last Word* came out, the football coach demanded an immediate apology from Mr. Hype and the assurance that a certain Jane Retton would not be permitted to write any more articles for the paper. The lady who oversaw the pep squads made similar demands. Mr. Hype told them to take a hike. "Miss Retton has written the first honest article about our dismal athletic department in years," he went on record as saying. Interfaculty squabbling naturally followed, dying out only when a compromise of sorts was reached. In the end Mr. Hype avoided making an apology, and Jane was allowed to stay on the paper on the condition she apply her shrewd analysis in any area except sports. This suited her just fine.

That was the official end of the matter. The guys on

the team continued to the present to corner her for
strategic advice, sometimes ganging up on her a dozen
at a time at lunch. As these attacks were all in fun, she
didn't mind.

The cheerleaders were another matter. They had
long memories. Patty had in fact promised her an
entire senior year of misery. Fortunately, the
confrontations had so far been purely verbal in na-
ture: making fun of Jane's clothes, ridiculing her car,
the usual jive. The only exception had occurred when
a dumpy baton twirler had jostled Jane's books out of
her book bag in the hallway. The incident might have
upset her if Sharon hadn't been with her and immediately thrown the Coke she was drinking in the girl's
face. The baton twirler had broken down and cried. So
far, there had been no major retaliation.

Jane wasn't losing any sleep over the matter. Patty
and the others would soon get bored with the whole
thing.

I'm hoping.

While Jane mused over the matter, Patty Brane
swept in and plopped down in the chair immediately
behind her. Two of her cheerleader chums took the
seats to Jane's immediate right and left. Patty had on a
red pants suit.

Kirk had been talking to Patty! She had touched
him!

"I've got a new lipstick for the game, Janey," Patty
said at her back. "Going to be looking awfully pretty
tonight. Hope you're planning on coming."

"I'm working," Jane said flatly, thinking, *Kirk can't
be interested in Patty. He has me. Why would he want
a tall curvaceous blonde who drops her pants at the
drop of a hat?*

Jane decided to stop thinking. She was depressing herself.

"It doesn't matter," Patty said, placing her black shoe next to Jane's arm, lightly dusting the sleeve of Jane's new white blouse. "You'll be seeing me all weekend. You and your *boy*friend. Will you be writing an article about our little adventure, by any chance?"

"Only if something exciting happens," Jane said.

Patty giggled and leaned so close that Jane could feel her gum-chewing breath on her cheek. "And what would you consider exciting? How about if I caught a big fish? And what if, say, I took this gorgeous fish to a secret part of the islands and ate my fill? Would that be worth putting in print, Janey?"

"I supposed if you choked on his bones, yes."

"Ah, *his* bones. The girl catches on quick." Patty chuckled, sat back. "You know, I like my fish raw."

"Fish are smarter than most people think." Jane turned slowly around. "They can usually smell where the water's polluted, where everyone's been dumping garbage. They know to stay away from such—places."

"Touché." Patty smiled, popping her gum as if she were cracking her knuckles, getting ready for a fight.

Just then, Jane looked up and saw Alice standing in the doorway of the studio, beckoning to her. That was odd; Alice was notoriously punctual, and the second bell was about to ring. Getting up, leaving her book bag behind, Jane made her way past the surrounding cheerleaders.

"I'm here to make sure Linda and Ralph know when to be at the dock," Alice explained, anticipating her question. "I've already checked in at my home-room. I've got a pass."

"But why go around now?" Jane asked. "Why not try to get everyone at break and lunch?"

Alice shook her head. "Half the seniors leave for the day at lunch. And at break, people are all over the place. I have a list of everyone's homeroom. I should be able to catch most of my guests in the next ten minutes." She glanced inside. "Oh, Patty's here. I can tell her about the time, too."

Jane pouted. "I think she already knows."

Alice was sympathetic. "Are they still hassling you?"

"I think Patty's after Kirk now."

A strange look touched Alice's normally soft expression. "Really? That's—" She didn't finish.

"What?"

"That doesn't surprise me. Look, stay here. When I confirm the invitation, I'll tell them my father doesn't want any bad feelings being carried aboard the boat."

"All right."

While Jane was waiting outside, Sharon appeared. "And what are you doing here?" Jane asked.

"I left my history book at home. I have it first period. Can I use yours? What's the combination to your locker? I can never remember it."

"My history book's in my bag inside. Go get it."

The second bell rang. "Why are you standing out here? Afraid there's going to be an earthquake?"

Jane nodded toward her homeroom. "Alice is in there pleading a truce with Patty on my behalf. I thought it would be too humiliating to be present while she did so."

"Why call a truce?" Sharon asked, stepping past her. "Why don't we just drown the rah-rahs this weekend?"

Alice came out then, having completed her invitations—Patty had nodded politely at her suggestion, Alice said—and Sharon returned with Jane's book. Both girls disappeared in opposite directions. Jane reentered her homeroom, choosing a seat in the back while the teacher called the roll and covered the day's announcements. When the next bell rang ten minutes later, Jane waited until Patty and pals had left and then went to collect her books.

Although Jane didn't know it then, she was already in deep trouble.

— CHAPTER III —

FIRST AND SECOND PERIODS PASSED UNEVENTFULLY. DUR-
ing break, Jane saw neither Alice nor Sharon nor Kirk.
She was finishing the last thirty pages of a mystery
romance and she just had to know whether the guy
would save the girl before the villain could waste them
both. Through all of the snack period, she stayed in
the library. It turned out the guy did rescue the girl.
Regrettably, the girl turned out to be the real villain,
and she killed the guy. Not a very cheery story.

The first hint of trouble came in third period. The
class was journalism, and Jane had composed an
editorial on how unfair it was that conservative
groups were able to have certain books banned
in some school districts. It was her hope to run
the article in the next issue of *The Last Word*.
Jane thought the work a fairly serious treatment
of an important topic. She didn't understand why
half the class burst out laughing when she finished
reading it.

If third period was odd, fourth belonged in the
Twilight Zone. History was the subject—Sharon never had returned her book—and all Jane could do was
sit and take notes on a boring fifty-minute lecture. Not

once did she raise her hand and ask a question, nor did the teacher ask her anything. In no way did she call special attention to herself. And yet most of the people in the room kept glancing her way, smiling at her.

Am I getting paranoid or what?

Jane began to check her clothes to see if anything was showing that shouldn't have been. Since she had on pants and a blouse, there wasn't much to check. Then she began to worry about her face. Perhaps someone had stamped her forehead with a lewd comment. Although this seemed highly unlikely, she went so far as to slip a tiny round mirror from her purse and study her reflection. Nope, nothing wrong there. Jane Retton had not changed.

Has the world? Is everyone going nuts?

The bell for lunch rang and she headed straight for the rest room. Another personal examination—a far more thorough one this time—uncovered nothing out of place. But as she stepped into the hallway, a friend of hers, Kathy Lingren, passed by, and the brief conversation that followed did nothing to ease Jane's mind.

"Hi, Kathy, what's up?"

"Nothing. How are you?" Kathy smiled at her, exactly as everyone else had been smiling the last couple of hours. "What have you been up to?"

"Nothing new."

Kathy burst out laughing. "Really?"

Jane felt a mild tremble inside. "What is it?"

"You crack me up. You're so mellow. I wonder what you would consider new in your life."

"What are you talking about?"

"Come off it, you know. How's Kirk?"

42

"How's Kirk? Kirk's fine. What does he have to do with— Why are you laughing?"

Kathy paused, taking a breath. "You really don't know why?"

"No. What's happened?"

Every trace of humor vanished from Kathy's face. It happened so suddenly the tremble inside Jane transformed itself into a full-fledged shake. "Oh, no. You don't know."

Jane swallowed. "Tell me."

Kathy turned away, shook her head. "I've got to go."

"Tell me!"

"It's nothing. I can't—Good-bye."

"Kathy?"

"Ask someone else," she called back over her shoulder.

It can't be that bad. Everyone seems to think it's funny.

Because everyone thought she knew what it was.

All of a sudden, Jane didn't feel terribly well. Alice and Sharon—they'd know what was going on. Looking around, looking for a direction to take, Jane set off at a brisk pace.

And everywhere she went, people *watched* her.

Patty Brane got to her, cornering her on the far side of the gym, before her friends could break the news gently. Jane had headed to the spot because Alice had P.E. before lunch and often practiced her tennis strokes alone against the smooth gym walls after everyone else had already showered. No one in the school could touch Alice at tennis.

But Alice had skipped extra practice that day. The place was deserted.

"Janey," Patty called, coming up behind her, moving like the hot stuff she thought she was. She must have been following her. "Looking for me?"

"No. Go away."

"Come on, be sociable. I'm here to help you."

Jane scowled. "The day I need your help, I'll be putting a gun to my head."

"Don't speak too soon." Patty hardened, thrusting a page at her. "Read this."

It was an eight-by-eleven page covered with neat handwriting, obviously a photocopy that had been made on the school's machine; the contraption was notoriously sloppy, and faint ink marks traced the edges of the paper.

Jane only had to read a few lines.

October 6th (138 days of high school left and counting)
Dear Diary,
I've been very naughty. I've gone and done what no good girl should do. I've lost my virginity. And I know exactly where I lost it. But let me tell you, there's no getting it back. . . .

The entire last page from her diary.

Jane died inside a little, maybe a lot. It must have been death of a sort, for she suddenly felt separate from her body. Yet she remained aware of the pain swelling in her chest. It was the pain that had driven her slightly out of her body. Her heart literally felt as if it would rupture.

"There're dozens of these copies floating around, Janey."

Jane coughed thickly, desperately trying to think. "Who wrote this?"

Patty grinned. The whole school grinned behind her. "It's your handwriting. Don't deny it."

Jane took a breath. The air had ashes in it. "It's a forgery."

"Hah!"

"Anybody could have imitated my handwriting." She wadded up the page. Yet she didn't throw it on the floor. She feared the janitor might find it later and take it home to his wife, who might have lunch with the mayor's wife on Sunday, who might then tell . . .

"You wrote it."

"Not me, I don't have that filthy an imagination." Patty laughed. "If I had any doubts it was genuine, you've just settled them. You may not realize it, but you're the cutest shade of green."

"You can't prove I wrote this."

"Do I have to?"

Jane hesitated. Patty had a point there. Whenever a lie was more scandalous than the truth, the public would believe the lie every time. "My name isn't even mentioned on this page."

"Kirk's is. Several times. And who else is going out with him?" Patty shook with excitement. "Anyway, Kirk's already told me all this really happened."

"Wha-what do you mean?"

"He said he slept with you last Saturday."

"You're lying."

"Ask him."

The pain kept getting worse and worse. "He didn't say that. Why would he say that?"

"You know guys. Scoring with a chick is better than

45

scoring a touchdown during a game. They're proud of it. They tell everybody. But don't be too hard on him. At least he didn't write about it."

Honest words had a definable ring to them, even when coming out of the mouth of a witch. Blood pounded behind Jane's eyes. "Who printed these?"

Patty held up her hand and slowly rubbed her fingers together. Black marks stained the tips. "It's confidential."

"You did it."

"Now you prove it. I'm going to wash my hands, and in two minutes there won't be a way in hell you can go to the faculty and legally pin a smear job on me."

"But you used the school's machine."

"It sure is tucked in a corner, isn't it? Who knows who's used it, and when?"

Jane asked *the* question. "Where did you get the original page?"

Triumph filled Patty's face. "From your diary."

"I don't have a diary."

"Then I guess you wouldn't be interested in the yellow notebook lying in our homeroom."

Jane almost blacked out. "No," she moaned.

"I'm afraid so. Better hurry before more pages are copied."

Jane had to struggle to keep standing. "You—you won't get away with this."

Patty leaned close. "Janey, old buddy, I already have."

Jane discovered the diary resting on the seat she had first occupied when she had entered her homeroom that morning. It was closed, but a page had been torn out and hastily replaced, the page Patty had photocopied.

Dear Diary— How could you do this to me?

Jane sat down, lowered her face to her arms, and began to cry.

CHAPTER IV

ALICE AND SHARON FOUND HER LATER. IT MIGHT HAVE BEEN much later, or only moments—Jane didn't know. Time was out of control. Each minute that passed expanded the circle of people who knew her most secret fantasies. She tried to imagine what that meant and couldn't. She couldn't imagine anything anymore. It was over, the whole shot.

I'll walk into the ocean and take a long deep drink. Might as well.

"How are you, kid?" Alice asked softly, sitting beside her, touching her shoulder. Jane glanced up, feeling dried tears across her cheeks. Alice's face was compassionate. Sharon stood behind her, looking more confused than anything else.

"You saw it?" Jane whispered.

Alice nodded, solemn. "Yeah."

"It's all over the place," Sharon said.

"Shh!" Alice hissed. "Show some tact."

"Sorry," Sharon muttered.

Jane closed her eyes, opened them. The world would not go away. "What's happening? Why— This can't be happening."

Alice gave her a hug. "It's not a pretty situation, I

won't fool you. But maybe you can head off a lot of the damage. Talk to Kirk. Have him deny it."

"Pretend you made up the whole thing," Sharon added.

"I did make up the whole thing," Jane said. They nodded in understanding, but not in belief. "I did! You two know me. I just wrote it as a joke."

"I thought it was sort of funny," Sharon said, trying to help and failing miserably. Alice chose to ignore her this time.

"Better hurry, Jane," she said. "The sooner Kirk starts telling others that this is just a smear job, the sooner it will blow over."

"But you two believe me, don't you? It's all a lie. Patty printed them up. She still has the Xerox toner on her hands."

"It doesn't matter what we believe," Alice began. "We're your friends. What—"

"It does matter!" Jane cried. "I didn't do it!"

"Jane, it was in your handwriting," Alice said gently.

"Okay, fine. So what? I've already admitted I wrote it. It just isn't true."

Sharon squinted. "This wasn't an article you were writing for one of those men's magazines, was it?"

"Sharon," Alice said, beginning to lose patience. "I think it would be best if you didn't speak for the next five minutes." She went on, "Jane, go now. Kirk has as much to lose by this whole thing as you. He'll help."

The advice appeared sound. But when Jane went to get up, it struck her that something very big and very important was being overlooked. Simply the thought of it was enough to chill her blood. She stared at her friends for a long moment. "How did my diary end up in Patty's hands?" she asked slowly.

"I don't know," Alice said.

"Sharon?" Jane asked.

"Can I speak?"

"Speak," Alice said.

"I don't know."

Jane kept her eyes on Sharon, who had begun to fidget. "I left my diary open on my desk. You went in my room to go to the bathroom. You were in there a long time."

"Jane, don't start accusing Sharon. She—"

"She was in there for fifteen minutes! Come on, Sharon, what took you so long?"

Sharon swallowed, frightened. "You know I would never hurt you. You know I—"

"All I know is the whole damn school is reading my diary! Now, did you bring it to school or not?"

"No."

"You're lying! You were in the room and—"

"Jane, I went into the room, too," Alice interrupted.

Jane stopped. "When?"

"When I went to get Sharon. I saw an open notebook lying on your desk. Was that your diary?"

"Yes, did you read it?"

"No, I didn't read it," Alice said, not offended. "I was in a hurry to get to school, remember? I went into the room, told Sharon we were leaving, and then she opened the door and we rejoined you in the other bathroom."

"Why did you leave your diary lying open on your desk?" Sharon asked.

"I was interrupted. The cat interrupted me."

"I didn't know you had a cat," Sharon said.

"I have a bunny. The cat was trying to eat the bunny!" She sighed, sitting back. "I forgot I'd left the diary out. I'd gotten a big shock when I saw what was happening outside in the backyard." Then she shook her head. "But this doesn't explain how my diary got into Patty's hands."

"I was hurrying both of you," Alice said. "If your diary is an ordinary notebook, isn't it possible you accidentally picked it up and put it in your bag with the rest of your books?"

"That's impossible," Jane said quickly.

"I thought I saw a yellow notebook in your bag when we were in the car," Sharon said. "Or maybe Alice had one."

"And how did you know it was a yellow notebook?" Jane demanded. "It was lying open on the desk. The outside covers weren't visible."

"Ah, I don't know."

"You can usually tell what color a notebook is even when its covers are face down," Alice said.

"No, you can't," Jane said. "Can you?"

"I think so," Alice said.

"But Sharon believes you might have been carrying it," Jane said, hating the suspicion in her voice almost as much as the suspicion in her mind. In response, Alice slipped a yellow spiral notebook from beneath her schoolbooks.

"I've had it since the first day of school."

Jane shook her head again. "All right, fine. But none of this answers the question. How did Patty get it?"

Alice grimaced suddenly. "It might have been my fault."

"What?" Jane snapped.

"I called you out of the room, remember? She must have noticed it in your bag then, and grabbed it."

"Why would Patty suddenly start going through my bag looking for a diary she didn't even know existed?" Jane threw Sharon another sharp glance. "But you had a reason to go through my books, didn't you?"

"I didn't see your diary," Sharon said. "I didn't do anything wrong. Now quit accusing Alice and me. We're trying to help you."

Alice nodded. "Patty was probably looking in your bag for anything she might swipe or mess up. Finding your diary was just bad luck. In either case, it's done. You have to deal with it. Talk to Kirk. Do it now, before lunch is over."

Jane leaned back, pressing her palms against her eyes; they were ready to explode out of their sockets. "I'm sorry. You're right, I must have—gotten messed up. Easter was bleeding, and then you two were at the door, and then I ran and grabbed my books and—" She stopped, weary, stumbling to her feet. "I'll try to find Kirk."

"We'll go with you," Alice said, taking her arm.

"Thank you. But I want to talk to him alone."

Before she could get to Kirk, Mr. Pan grabbed her. Mr. Pan doubled as the psych teacher and senior class counselor. Friendly and helpful to the point of being bothersome, he was always trying to get problem students to "open up" to him. During the last four years, Jane had never heard of a single student who had opened up enough to satisfy Mr. Pan's quest for total honesty. She thought he would be more at home on a radio talk show.

"Jane," he said, appearing out of nowhere as they

were hurrying down the hallway. "I'd like you to come to my office for a few minutes."

"She can't, not now," Alice said.

"She has to study," Sharon said.

"I think what we have to discuss is more important than your studying," Mr. Pan said, moving across their path, blocking their way. He had been a hippie in the sixties, and although he now wore his sandy hair short—what was left of it—and bought his clothes at finer stores, he still tried to maintain a "hip" air. He never buttoned the top button on his shirt, and he had a fetish for blue sneakers.

"Does it have to be now?" Jane asked.

He put a hand on her shoulder. Touching was one of his favorite ways of communicating. "I want to help."

"Can my friends come?"

"I'd rather they didn't." He glanced at Alice and Sharon. "No offense meant."

"None taken," Sharon said.

Alice smiled politely. "We're coming."

Five minutes later the three girls were sitting in Mr. Pan's office. Perhaps he felt a kinship with the fairy god who shared his last name; he had flowered fields shot through with tacky psychedelic rainbows for wallpaper. The colors didn't help Jane's growing headache.

"I've seen this," he said gravely, bringing forth a copy of her diary entry.

"Hasn't everybody?" Jane muttered. Next she expected to hear a phony discourse on how sympathetic he was to the emotional suffering she must be going through. He caught her completely by surprise.

"I admire your honesty, Jane."

"Huh?"

He sat back, reaching for a bottle of Perrier, offering them the same. They shook their heads. He went on, "It's rare to find a young woman who can express her feelings with such openness and—this was especially impressive to me—such wit."

Jane almost gagged. "What are you talking about? You think I wrote that for the whole school to read?"

He raised an eyebrow, mildly surprised. "Who you wrote it for isn't important to me. The fact that you did write it is what matters."

"But I didn't write it," Jane said. "Someone else did. They're trying to humiliate me."

He sipped his overpriced water. "Really, Jane, it's nothing to be ashamed of. According to the latest surveys, fifty-three percent of the kids your age are having sex. It's a normal, natural activity. Actually, after having read what you wrote, I'm surprised to hear you talking this way. You sounded truly at home with your own sensuality."

"At home with my sensuality?" Jane said, incredulous.

"Did you do it at home?" Sharon asked her.

"Mr. Pan," Alice said, "I don't think this discussion is what Jane needs right now. You seem to be completely ignoring the fact that something extremely private about her has been exposed for public ridicule. And, furthermore, I don't believe it's proper for you to be talking alone with three girls about sex."

Mr. Pan sat up. "Very well, I apologize if I have not shown the proper sympathy. I didn't know this paper had been circulated without Jane's knowledge. Tell me, Jane, how did that happen?"

"It was my bunny's fault," she growled.

The comment didn't faze him. "I see. Well, I

wouldn't worry too much about it. Indeed, the copies will probably enhance your popularity in some respects." He cleared his throat. "I want to get to the reason I brought you here, but first let me address Alice's second objection: I wholly disagree that it is outside my prerogative as your counselor to discuss sex with you three. If you don't learn the facts of life at home and they're not taught at school, where does that leave you?"

"Without a date," Sharon said, then laughed. "Never mind. Just a joke. Sorry."

"There's an element of truth in what you have just said," Mr. Pan went on seriously. "But there is another issue even more important than dating." He paused, leaned toward Jane. "Do you know what I'm getting at?"

"I haven't the foggiest," Jane said, glancing out the window. The courtyard was visible from where she sat, and it seemed to her that dozens of single-sheet photocopies were being passed from hand to hand, although in truth she could see none.

Give her time, Patty will make a poster out of it.

"Teenage pregnancy," Mr. Pan said grimly.

"Oh, God," Sharon said.

"I'm not pregnant," Jane said sharply.

"Are you sure?" Mr. Pan asked. "I couldn't help noticing in your recollection of that night that you didn't mention contraceptives. Tell me honestly, Jane, are you using any?"

"Any what? No, I'm not. Why should I? I'm not having sex!"

"Mr. Pan," Alice broke in, "I really think we'd better go."

The counselor had opened the bottom drawer of his

desk and was taking out two small cardboard boxes. "I bought these myself. I want you to have them. I want you to read the instructions on the side and use them." He looked at her with all sincerity. "I don't want you messing up your life, Jane, with a silly mistake."

"They're free?" Sharon asked.

Jane stood. "I'm getting out of here."

Alice also got up. "I'm sorry, Mr. Pan, but I feel you're way out of line."

"Now wait a sec," Sharon said. "If he's giving them away free, I don't see what you're both complaining about." She picked up one of the boxes. "Are these like samples, or are they the real thing?"

"They're real; they work," Mr. Pan said, also getting to his feet, trying to press a box into Jane's hand. "Please, for my peace of mind, take them and take care of yourself."

Jane shook off his offer. "Leave me alone!"

He took a step back. "I understand this is all new for you, and it must sound crude to be talking about it. Don't worry. I will keep them for now, and when you're ready you can come to me. In fact, I'll take them with me on our trip this weekend."

"You're coming?" Alice asked, astounded.

Mr. Pan beamed. "Yes, your father wanted a faculty member present, and I was elected. It should be lots of fun." He glanced again at Jane, added seriously, "As long as some of us use common sense."

Jane ran from the room.

Kirk had a group of about a dozen guys around him. They were standing outside next to the punch machine, one of the busiest places on campus. Lunch hour was nearly over. Kirk didn't seem to be in much pain. The gang around him mostly wore smiles.

"Are you sure you don't want us to go with you?" Alice asked.

"I'm sure," Jane said, leaving her friends behind, striding directly into the group, looking neither right nor left. The boys fell silent as she approached, no big favor. Lewd remarks would have been easier to handle; she knew they would start up the instant she left.

"Jane," Kirk said, startled by her sudden appearance.

She nodded toward the parking lot. "Over there, let's talk."

They weren't even out of earshot when the guys started giggling.

"What happened?" she asked when they were relatively alone.

"What do you mean?"

"Patty says you told her we slept together last Saturday."

Kirk wiped at his mouth, then put his hands in his pockets and rocked back on his heels. "I don't remember saying that."

He won't look me in the eye! Could it be true?

"What do you remember?" she demanded, her tone undergoing a drastic change. Not for an instant had she actually believed Patty. "If what Patty said is even remotely true, then you're quicker than any guy on campus 'cause I didn't feel a thing."

"Jane, you're mad."

"No. I'm just dying of joy to hear about this love life of mine I didn't even know I had. Of course I'm mad!

The whole world thinks I'm a slut! My counselor is trying to give me condoms! And I'm still a virgin! Did you tell Patty we slept together or not?"

He lowered his head. "No."

"You're lying!" She had shouted the same words at Sharon minutes ago.

"I'm not." He folded his arms across his chest, still avoiding her gaze. "Did you write that page?"

Patty had not shown him the entire diary. "No."

"It looked like your handwriting?"

"Did you tell Patty that?"

"No. Well, yes. She showed it to me before I had a chance to read it. She asked if it looked like a paper you had lost." He paused, his face miserable. "I'm sorry."

"Then did she let you read it?"

He nodded.

"Then what did you tell her, exactly?"

"I didn't say we'd had sex."

"What did you tell her?"

"Nothing."

"What?"

"I didn't say anything."

"You didn't deny that it was true?"

"I didn't think it was any of my business."

Jane hurt so bad she had to laugh. "None of your business? The damn thing was about you!"

"Then you did write it?"

"Yes! Are you happy now? I wrote it this morning. But what difference does that make? Why didn't you tell her it was fake? You might have stopped it right then and there."

"Well, you did say that one line: 'Gimme a kiss.' I remembered that."

"And you told her that?"

"I didn't want to lie. I mean, I thought you wrote it, and I didn't want to make you look like a liar. That's what I mean."

"You're either the biggest idiot on the entire West Coast, or else I am for going with you. I—" Jane caught herself, remembering.

"You know guys. Scoring with a chick is better than scoring a touchdown during a game. They're proud of it. They tell everybody. . . ."

The fury that started to burn in Jane in that instant took her a long way from the numbness that had overcome her with the original discovery. It pushed her into a place where she had never been before, a dark place where hate made many impossible things not only possible but desirable.

Patty had spread the word, true, but Kirk, her *boyfriend,* had given the word strength.

Jane's voice was like ice. "You didn't deny it because you wanted everyone to think it was true."

"No, that's not so."

"It is."

"Hey, you're being unfair. *You're* the one who wrote it." He looked at her for the first time. "Why did you?"

"You're right, why did I?"

"Jane—"

"You're never going to kiss me again."

"But—"

She slapped him across the face, hard enough to snap his head back. Her hand stung with pain and she welcomed it. "Never," she repeated, leaving him with blood trickling from his nose. The blood reminded her of the red spots on Easter, of her lingering anxiety about the cat. Perhaps her subconscious had been trying to warn her of another monster that was about to pounce. Or perhaps the blood had been an omen of things to come.

Jane left the school without speaking to Alice and Sharon. She walked all the way home. And on the way, she thought of how to make them pay.

CHAPTER V

JANE WENT TO WORK THAT AFTERNOON. SHE FELT IT WOULD be better than sitting at home waiting for obscene phone calls. Besides, her parents had said they would give her a call when they were settled; they'd expect her to be at work. She hadn't had a chance to consider how they would take the news. That they would hear about it appeared inevitable. Especially when she got to work and discovered that Dr. Palmer had already been given the big scoop. Alice hadn't told him; seemed a kid from school had been in during lunch hour to have her teeth cleaned. She had blabbed the whole story.

Dr. Palmer had not raised the issue so far, except to ask if she wanted to work in the back with the files for the whole afternoon. Normally, that was Alice's job. Jane usually played receptionist: greeting people, collecting money, writing receipts, and scheduling appointments. For all her beauty and manners, Alice had never been very good at handling the public. She had a tendency to stiffen up when she talked to strangers.

Jane accepted Dr. Palmer's offer and buried herself in the back room, sorting X-rays and their accompanying paperwork, searching for old records to be stored outside the office, trying to keep busy so she wouldn't have to think too far ahead.

Beside her on the desk lay a small notepad. On it she had written an unusual collections of notes:

1. Kill P. and K.
2. Cripple K.
3. Disfigure P.
4. Infect P. and K. with incurable disease.
5. Disgrace P. and K.

People often spoke of getting revenge. But when you got right down to it, Jane realized, there were only a few things you could do to someone. Given their age, ruining either Kirk or Patty financially wasn't worth mentioning. And when she studied the list critically, all but one option disappeared.

Sure, she could conceivably devise a scheme to either mess them up or wipe them out altogether. Unfortunately, the police would immediately target her as the prime suspect. More than anything, she wanted to avoid other people right now, but jail wasn't her idea of a nice place to do it.

Number four did have a certain charm. Obtaining a blood sample of someone with a transmittable disease was not out of the question. But keeping the blood fresh and deadly until she could secretly inject it into their systems would be next to impossible.

And I might catch it myself.

Of course she couldn't kill anybody. She wasn't crazy.

That left number five. Leaving school, her thoughts had instinctively turned in the direction of ruining their reputations, as they had ruined hers. An eye for an eye—that was fair. And already she had the outline of a plot so devilishly clever she could hardly believe she had thought it up. On the one hand, it had a single flaw: the damage wouldn't be permanent. On the other hand, for a couple of days, they would suffer awfully. She must be a genius.

Jane tore her list into a thousand pieces.

No more incriminating evidence.

A pity she would have to confide in Sharon before her plot could ripen, but it couldn't be helped. One of the girls would have to know, and telling Alice would surely be a mistake; she would try to talk her out of it. Sharon it would have to be.

"My father wants to see you," Alice called, coming to the door.

"What for?" Jane asked, tensing. First Mr. Pan's contraceptives and now probably a lecture on morality.

"I don't know." Alice stepped inside. "How are you doing?"

"I've found over a hundred files we no longer need to keep here."

"No, I mean are you okay?"

Jane stood. For no reason, the question bugged her. "I'm fine. Where's your dad?"

"In Room Three."

Alice followed her into the room. Dr. Palmer was bent over, tinkering with a valve on an anesthesic bottle. Seen from that angle, his behind sticking in the air, he was literally wider than he was tall. Jane didn't know how someone who didn't eat white sugar could get so fat.

"Blasted thing's a week old and it's already losing pressure. Angel, where did you put . . . ?" He stopped, seeing he wasn't alone with his daughter. "Oh, Jane, yes. I want to have a word with you."

"I'll wait outside," Alice said.

"Just a moment," Dr. Palmer said, straightening up. "Have a look at this. I'm not getting a smooth flow of gas."

Alice studied the equipment for a moment. "The anesthesic's fine," she said finally. "It's the oxygen line that's the problem. These new valves begin to close again when you turn them too far."

"Since when?"

"The manufacturer explained about the change in the new literature. Remember, I showed you?"

"You showed me no such thing."

Alice lowered her voice. "I must have forgotten."

Dr. Palmer chuckled. "Isn't this wonderful, Jane? All my years of education, and I have to depend on my daughter to tell me how to use my equipment." He nodded toward Alice. "Please close the door on your way out."

When she was gone, Dr. Palmer gestured toward a chair. "Have a seat, Jane; make yourself comfortable." She did as she was told. He leaned against the counter, regarding her with what he probably intended to be a we-can-talk expression, but which said to her she had better move carefully.

"How long have you and Alice known each other?" he asked.

"About a year."

"You've become good friends in that time, haven't you?"

"Yes."

He nodded. "I hope you stay friends. I think you're good for each other. And I like having you in the office. You're great with the patients. Many times I've had them comment to me on how you make them feel at home when they enter the office, how you get them to relax when they're anxious about their treatment. Those are rare abilities, Jane, and I value them. I wanted you to know that."

"Thanks."

He scratched his head. "But I've got a problem I need your help with. I think you know what I'm talking about."

He thinks he's got a problem.

"Yes, sir. But I don't want you to worry about it. I'll handle it."

He shook his head sadly. "I'm afraid it's not that simple. What you've done—it has far-reaching implications."

"But, sir, I haven't done anything. The page that was circulated at school was—"

"Now, now, dear," he interrupted. "I may be old-fashioned, but I haven't lived the last twenty years with my head stuck in the sand. I read the papers and watch the news. I know the life-styles of today's teenagers are not what they were when I was in high school. We can be frank with each other."

"I am being frank. I haven't done anything wrong. I haven't done anything, period."

He frowned, sharpening his tone. "That's not what I wanted to hear. It may seem like nothing in your eyes, but let me tell you, girl, if it were my daughter we were talking about, you could be sure her punishment would be of the sort she wouldn't soon forget."

Jane stared at him in disbelief. His perspective was a hundred and eighty degrees in the other direction from Mr. Pan's, and they sounded exactly the same.

Why try to convince either of them? They were happy where they were.

"How can I help you?" she asked, hiding her sarcasm so well that Dr. Palmer softened his voice and smiled.

"That's better. Let's not dwell on the past. Let's discuss what we can do to improve the future, *your* future." He pulled up a chair and sat by her side. "Do you know, Jane, what it means to be strong?"

"I think so."

"It means not to give in to impulse. To weigh the results of a course of action before taking it. It means to respect your body, to put that respect above all carnal desire. Do you understand what I am trying to tell you?"

Don't screw around. That's obvious.

"Yes, sir."

"I hope you do. It's important to me, not only because I want to keep you on as an employee, but because Alice listens to you. She's influenced by what you do. And you know how much my angel means to me, don't you?"

"I do."

"Also, I'm a health professional. I know about the things that are going around today."

"The things?"

He nodded gravely. "Boys can give you these things. You have to be careful, always on your guard, always strong. Are you listening to me?"

"Yes, sir."

"And you'll be good? You must promise me you will."

"I promise."

He hugged her. "You're a beautiful girl, Jane. Your

heart hasn't been poisoned by any of this. I can see that. That's the reason I've decided to keep you on."

God, he was considering firing me!

"Thank you."

He stood. "You can go now. Work hard tonight and have fun this weekend. You're still coming with us, aren't you?"

"Sure." She got up. "Dr. Palmer, could I ask you a favor?"

"You most certainly may."

"Can Kirk Donner come on the trip?" She continued quickly as he started to shake his head. "Please? I feel if he could hear what you just told me it would make a big difference. I could tell him myself, but coming from you it would have so much more authority. Please?"

He considered. "Very well, if you feel it will help straighten out his life. But I know Kirk. He's low class. I've spoken to him in the past, and it was like talking to a stone. I strongly advise you never to see him again."

"After this weekend, I don't think I will."

Sharon came in an hour later. By then Jane had pulled and sorted another fifty records. The manila folders holding the X-rays were stacked high over every available inch of table space. Sharon immediately picked one up.

"Jeez, these are gross, all these teeth and bones and stuff," she said. "Wonder if I look like that inside? Guess I must. Makes you want to puke when you think about it, doesn't it?"

"Do you want to see your own X-rays?" Jane asked. Sharon was one of Dr. Palmer's patients. Getting her teeth cleaned was an ordeal for her. She had a low pain threshold.

"No! What if I look and there's this big honking tumor eating away my jaw? No, thanks, no way."

"I suppose you're wondering why I called you in?"

Sharon shrugged. "I assumed you were feeling low and needed a pep talk. I don't blame you. If it had happened to me, I probably would have killed myself by now."

"Funny you should say that. Could you close the door, Sharon?"

Sharon did as requested and then sat beside Jane at the cluttered table. "What's up?"

"I'm going to get back at Kirk and Patty."

Sharon was interested. "How?"

"I'm going to have them kill me."

"Huh?"

"I'll explain in a moment. But first I want you to swear to me that what I say in this room will stay in this room. You can't even tell Alice, not now."

— CHAPTER VI —

In the Room

"SHARON TOLD YOU ANYWAY?" LIEUTENANT FISHER asked.

"Yes," Alice said. "But not until it was too late to stop Jane."

Fisher glanced at his watch: two-twelve. They had been at it an hour. Once he had gotten her going, Alice had talked freely, requiring little prodding. Her memory for details was remarkable. She could recount whole portions of conversations. Listening, Fisher had begun to build up a picture of the personalities involved. Even the elusive Jane Retton had begun to take shape in his mind. Yet Alice herself remained a mystery, and she was only an arm's length away. She could describe everyone's feelings throughout the confusion except her own. On the other hand, she didn't appear indifferent to the events. There was a pain in her voice that she couldn't have faked.

His drowsiness had vanished. He had a feeling he would have trouble sleeping for the next week. He had taken a lot of notes.

"Before you tell me about Jane's plan, I'd like to backtrack for a moment. I'm still confused about how the diary got into Patty's hands?"

A note of wariness entered Alice's voice. "What do you mean?"

"From all that you've said, Jane has struck me as a cautious young woman. Now, I understand fully how the rabbit getting attacked could momentarily make her forget about the diary. But to accidentally take the notebook to school—that's something else."

Alice shifted uncomfortably. "There was something I didn't mention."

"You read the diary while it was sitting on Jane's desk?"

Her eyes widened. "How did you know?"

Fisher smiled. "Probably most of us pride ourselves on not being nosy, but you only have to look at the sales figures for the *Enquirer* and the *Star* to realize we are a society of gossips. Don't feel bad, I peeped at my girlfriend's diary once. Wish I hadn't, though."

"Why?"

"There was nothing about me in it," he lied. His girlfriend didn't even keep a diary, and if she had, he wouldn't have dared invade her privacy. But Alice smiled, relaxing a bit, and he continued, "Tell me about it?"

"I didn't mean to look at it. When I entered the room, it was just sitting there, right out in the open. I glanced at it—I read very quickly—and I think I was halfway down the page before I realized what I was doing." She hesitated. "I felt awful about it afterward."

"Did Sharon catch you in the act?"

"No."

"Do you think Sharon read it also?"

"Yes. But Sharon didn't touch it."

"What do you mean, touch it? Did you pick it up or what?"

"Well, like I said, I felt guilty. And I felt embarrassed for Jane. I closed the diary and put it aside." She winced. "I put it in a terrible place. I didn't mean to."

"Where did you put it?"

"On top of her schoolbooks."

"Oh, I see. And that's how Jane ended up accidentally taking it to school?"

She nodded, tugging nervously at her long black hair. "It was all my fault. I wish now I had told Jane the truth. Maybe none of this would have happened."

The explanation was more logical than the original one; nevertheless, Fisher felt unsatisfied. Not for the first time, he wished they could locate Sharon. "Don't blame yourself. No one could have predicted what would happen. But let's go on. I'm curious about Kirk. I'm not clear why he helped ruin Jane's reputation. She was, after all, his girl."

Alice stared at him strangely. "Guys are always pulling stunts like that."

He had touched a nerve. "Did Kirk ever pull a stunt like that on you?"

"No. I wouldn't have stood for it."

"Apparently you didn't stand for something about Kirk. You did break up with him."

"I told you already, we didn't get along."

"Could you be more specific?"

"He wasn't my type. He never thought about the future, getting ahead, stuff like that. He was lazy."

"Why did you go out with him in the first place?"

"He asked me."

Fisher considered a moment. "Alice, was Kirk the first boy to ever ask you out?"

"No. I mean, he was the first one who asked me after I was allowed to date. But I used to get asked out before then. I just never went."

"When did your dad start letting you date?"

"On my seventeenth birthday."

"Isn't that sort of late?"

"I don't know."

"Was there anything else you didn't like about Kirk?"

She was slow in answering. "Not really."

"Weren't you even a little jealous that your old boyfriend was going out with your best friend?"

"No." She sounded as if she meant it.

"All right. Tell me Jane's plan."

"It was crazy, brilliant—just like Jane. Maybe she stole part of it from a book she read—she was always reading books—but I don't think so. I think she made it all up in her head.

"As I said, she wanted to make it look as if Kirk and Patty had accidentally killed her. If that happened, she figured they'd suffer from a lot of guilt and blame. Everyone would come down hard on them just as they were coming down on her.

"On our way to the islands, she planned to get Kirk and Patty together with her at the bow of the boat. Once there, she was going to start an argument with them, try to get both of them yelling at her. With Patty, she knew this would be easy, but Kirk was another matter. She realized she was really going to have to push him. You see, she needed one of them, preferably Kirk, to push her. I mean physically push her."

"Why?" Fisher asked.

"So she could fall off the boat and disappear."

"Come again?"

"Friday night, the night before the trip, Jane fastened scuba equipment to the rudder of the boat we were using. When she got pushed over the side, she was going to grab the equipment, start breathing the bottled air, and sink down to the bottom. Then she planned on changing into her full gear and swimming back to shore so that everyone would think she had drowned."

Fisher sat for a full minute digesting what Alice had just said. "Could this plan have worked?" he asked finally.

Alice nodded. "I think it did work. I think it worked too well."

"You don't know?"

"I haven't seen Jane since she went over the side."

"Of course you haven't." The revelation had thrown him off balance. That a girl still in high school would have the nerve to do such a thing seemed unbelievable.

Yet she did go into the water, and she never came out, he reminded himself, remembering his captain's summary of the official report of events aboard the boat.

Fisher shook his head. "They're too many flaws in this. Where did Jane get the scuba equipment?"

"She must have rented it. When she came on board, she had the equipment I had given her. I know that for a fact. She might have rented the other stuff out of town."

Fisher made a note. "We'll check on that. How was she able to sneak into the harbor at night, and how did

73

she attach the equipment to the bottom of the boat? They have security at that marina."

"Sharon told me she swam into the marina from the sea, part of the way underwater, dragging the equipment. Attaching it would have been easy. She could have used an ordinary screw clamp. You can buy them in sailing stores. I've used them before to dangle a camera from the bottom of our boat."

"But to circle into the harbor from outside with all that equipment—I would imagine that would require tremendous endurance."

"I could have done it, and Jane could outswim me any day."

"Wouldn't the scuba gear have upset the speed and direction of the boat once you were under way? Didn't your dad notice anything?"

Alice considered. "My father did think the boat was handling poorly, but he had never sailed her before, and we were just getting going. Our speed was slow."

"After Jane fell off the deck, how did she have time to get into all her equipment?"

"She didn't plan on getting into it right away. All she needed to do was open the valve on her tank, get hold of the mouthpiece, and sink to the bottom. Down there she could have taken all the time she wanted to put on her full gear."

"How deep is the water we're talking about?"

"About forty feet."

"Is that all? If this really happened, how come people on the boat weren't able to see her?"

"The sun wasn't all the way up yet. When the light's poor, you can't see someone ten feet under. Jane told Sharon she had the whole thing timed to the second, and I believe her. *I* couldn't see her from the boat."

"What about bubbles? Wouldn't they have given her away?"

"Good-size swells were coming at us from the north. They were glassy, but we had foam forming around the boat. That could easily have hidden a few bubbles. Plus when she didn't come up after a few seconds, we went looking for her. There were dozens of us splashing around. There was no way we would have spotted the air from her tank."

Fisher didn't scuba dive; he couldn't be absolutely sure the facts she was feeding him were accurate. But she sure seemed to know what she was talking about.

He began to feel a touch of admiration for Jane. But reality cut it off at the start. People were dead.

And I still don't know how or why.

"But Jane couldn't play dead indefinitely," he said. "What was the purpose in all this?"

"Her parents were gone for the weekend. She could have pretended to be dead at least that long. That would have been long enough to bring Kirk and Patty down."

"But didn't she consider all the trouble she would get into once everyone discovered she'd set them up?"

"Jane was never going to admit to anything. She was simply going to show up at school on Monday and say she'd swum back to shore and that we must have missed her."

"She was going to play dumb?"

"Yes."

"Why?"

"So she wouldn't get in trouble."

"No, I mean why do any of this?" he asked, finally letting his exasperation show. "Was what happened to her that awful?"

Alice gave him a rare look in the eyes. "When you're our age, there's nothing worse than being humiliated. Nothing."

There was a knock at the door. Officer Rick stuck his head in again. Fisher jumped up before he could speak and stepped into the hallway, closing the door at his back.

"Is it the father?" Fisher asked.

"He won't sit still much longer," Officer Rick said. "But the captain's doing a good job in that department, talking with him about the Bible and the meaning of life. You know Cap used to be in the ministry? I guess you would. How much longer do you need with the girl?"

"Maybe till the sun comes up."

Officer Rick held out an unsealed envelope. "This might speed things up for you. Dr. Hilt finished his preliminary examination. That body we found in the hills? It belongs to Jane Retton."

Fisher didn't accept the envelope. The pain he had felt earlier when looking at Jane's picture came back, only stronger, because now he knew about her and she was real to him.

She had been real.

"Hilt's sure?"

"Yeah, no question about it." The young officer wiped sweat from his brow. "I don't like this. A girl drowns out in the ocean and we find her body burned to a crisp up in the hills. What the hell's going on?"

"I wish I knew, buddy." Fisher leaned against the wall, his weariness suddenly returning. "Alice gave the impression we might find another body in the ashes."

"She said that?"

"She implied it. She may have been thinking of Sharon Less, but I'm not sure yet."

"I haven't heard anything. The captain called off examining the wreckage until we get some light."

"Tell the captain we can't wait. If our people have already left the area, send them back up. I don't want a single cinder of that house left unturned."

Officer Rick departed to carry out his order. Back in the room, alone once again with Alice, Fisher opened the yearbook and stared at the photograph of Jane, noting again her distracted expression, the faraway look in her eyes. Perhaps part of her had known she wouldn't be around all that long.

"What is it?" Alice asked.

Fisher sighed. "It was Jane's body."

Tears welled up in Alice's eyes. "I knew it must be," she whispered.

He closed the annual. "Let's go back to when Jane disappeared."

CHAPTER VII

THE SUN WOULD BE ALL THE WAY UP IN MINUTES. Although her night had seemed unending—she hadn't slept a wink—this was one dawn Jane wasn't anxious to greet. The remains of darkness above her head, the cold salt water beneath her bare feet—these were the cloaks she would wear as she entered the carefree land of make-believe death. She would wrap herself in them tightly before she allowed herself to rest.

Wild Wind rose and settled smoothly on the endless succession of four-foot northern swells, the huge boat effortlessly absorbing the thick waves. A faint spray fanned Jane as she sat alone on the foredeck. She was alone, but she knew she was being watched; she probably always would be.

But soon, for a little while at least, they'll watch someone else.

Jane tensed. The time was near. All her planning would now either give her the satisfaction of revenge or transform her into a bigger fool. Two things worried her: Sharon's role, and Kirk's reaction to her own fury. From the beginning, she had recognized her need for Sharon. When the big moment came, Sharon would have to tell Alice, quickly, that there was nothing to worry about. Jane had no intention of putting Alice through the agony of thinking she was dead. But let the rest of the class moan and groan.

If they do even that, the unfeeling bastards.

Sharon served another purpose. She was to bring Patty and Kirk to Jane when the time was right. It had, in fact, been Sharon who had called Kirk Friday evening to reassure him that his *girlfriend* still wanted him on the trip. Jane probably could have done it herself, but she had been afraid her temper would get the best of her. Kirk had been uncertain about boarding the boat, Sharon had told her later, but there he was, hanging out with the gang. He hadn't approached her yet, and for that she was grateful.

He's afraid. He should be afraid.

The Santa Barbara Islands lay twenty miles off their bow, hilly gray strips of land alternately appearing and disappearing with the bobbing of the boat. Thin, motionless purple clouds hung above the islands; the sun would deal with them soon enough. It was going to be warm. Jane could feel the sweat forming beneath the wet-suit top she wore hidden beneath her bulky sweater. She'd have to discard the sweater once she reached the bottom. But she had on shorts, and they would fit comfortably beneath the rest of the wet suit, which waited for her, along with all the scuba gear, only a few wet feet away.

Jane glanced back the way they had come, in the direction of the marina. They were about a mile out, which was sufficient for her needs. She had scuba dived with Alice in this very spot the past spring. She knew what to expect on the ocean floor. Sand and water.

Jane caught Sharon's eye, nodded slightly. Dressed in a bikini bottom and a green sweatshirt, Sharon hurried toward her.

"Do you know how weird you look sitting up here all alone?" Sharon asked in a loud whisper. "Everyone's looking at you."

"That's the point. Bring me my pals."

Sharon glanced nervously over her shoulder, showing the first signs of uncertainty. She'd almost burst with excitement when she first heard about the plan. "What if they don't come?"

"Do what I said and they'll come."

Sharon frowned. "What was that?"

Jane groaned. "Tell Patty I want to talk to her, that I know something she needs to know. Just tell Kirk I want to see him. Speak to Kirk first."

"What if you cramp while you're swimming back in?"

"I won't cramp."

"But you were up all night swimming. You must be tired."

"The only thing that's tiring me right now is you. Just do it." Jane stopped as Sharon's face fell. The stress must have gotten to her. She shouldn't have talked that way to one of her few remaining friends. "Look, I'm sorry. It's just that the longer we postpone, the farther out we get." She squeezed Sharon's hand. "Don't worry about me. When we get together later at your parents' cabin, you'll have the honor of meeting your first ghost."

Sharon smiled. "You amaze me, Jane. Did I ever tell you that?"

"I amaze myself." She nodded. "Now go, quickly. Remember to take care of Alice."

I'm talking as if I really am going to die.

Kirk had on blue jeans and a partially buttoned gray shirt that let his tanned chest show. After Sharon spoke to him, he approached slowly, his expression remorseful, at first avoiding Jane's eyes and then staring straight into them. For Jane it was like seeing him for the first time; no, like seeing him again after ages. There was a difference. A ripple of doubt, faint but spreading, touched her.

There wasn't a person on the boat who wasn't watching him.

He braved a faint smile, standing above her, steadying himself on one of the rigging lines. "How are you, Jane?"

"Fine. Didn't think I'd see you here." Out the corner of her eyes, she watched Sharon speaking to Patty.

"Sharon told me you wanted me to come." He obviously felt he was on thin ice. "Is that true?"

"Yeah."

"Does that mean you're not mad anymore?" he asked hopefully.

Now Patty was coming, bouncing and hopping in her chest-busting T-shirt like a good cheerleader should, wanting to discover what the defeated Jane Retton had on her mind. Seeing Patty's grin, realizing she would have to see it until June if she did nothing, and knowing Kirk was partly responsible for it, Jane hardened. "Not exactly," she said.

"Janey!" Patty exclaimed. "What a picture you make for us all sitting up here in the bow. What are you up to? Searching for sperm whales?"

"Patty," Kirk said nervously, "could you leave us alone for a few minutes?"

"But I've received an invitation to be here. Isn't that so?"

Jane slowly stood up. "Yeah, that's right. I've got something to tell the two of you." She paused. "You're both going to jail."

Kirk blinked. "What?"

Patty lost her smile for a second, then giggled. "I'm curious. Please go on."

"You're both legally adults. Libel and theft are serious crimes." She held up a hand, began to count on her fingers. "I have a witness who will swear in court that she saw Patty Brane making numerous copies of a single page on October sixth on the school's Xerox machine. I have another witness who can verify that on October sixth Patty Brane stole a yellow notebook from Jane Retton's book bag during homeroom. I have two witnesses who will swear that Jane Retton wasn't even in the company of Kirk Donner on the evening of September thirtieth, but was enjoying a movie with these two witnesses. I also have six witnesses who will verify that on the morning of October sixth, Patty Brane and Kirk Donner were seen talking and touching each other outside the science building."

Patty's eyes iced over. "B.S."

"J-Jane," Kirk stuttered, "why are you saying these things? We went out last Saturday. Don't you remember?"

"I remember nothing of the kind."

Patty took a step closer, trying to bore a hole in Jane's head with her stare. "You don't have a case."

"My family lawyer doesn't agree. He's handling the matter on a contingency basis. He figures with a third of the expected settlement, he will clean up on the Branes and the Donners."

"You're bluffing," Patty spat. "You're lying."

Patty had a point, but Jane was just getting warmed up. "My lawyer has also had the photocopies you made examined by an expert. This expert is ready to state in court that the handwriting on the so-called diary entry isn't mine."

Patty's temper sizzled. "If you have someone say I stole your notebook, you're admitting that I snatched a real page from your diary."

Jane shook her head confidently. "When combined with all the other evidence, it will be seen that you were merely preparing to set me up. Besides, if you admit you did steal something out of my bag, you'll be guilty before you can begin."

Patty started to speak, then thought better of it. She had fallen into the trap. Everything Jane had said so far could have been fabricated, but Patty couldn't be sure of that. Naturally, the bitch turned on Kirk. "You told me it was her handwriting!" she said.

"I thought it was." He was still trying to catch up on all the latest news. "Jane, I wasn't touching Patty. I was just talking to her. And we did go out last Saturday. I know we did."

Jane checked again to be sure they had the attention of the rest of the passengers. Dr. Palmer and Mr. Pan were watching them warily. She would have to pick up the tempo faster than she had anticipated. "You went out with Patty last Saturday?" she asked, raising her voice.

"No. I mean you and I did."

"We did what?" she yelled back. "Are you saying I slept with you?"

"No, I'm saying we—"

"Yes or no? Come on, say it! Who did you sleep with? It was this tramp here, wasn't it!"

"No—"

"Who are you calling a tramp?" Patty demanded. The threat of the lawsuit had, as Jane had hoped, rattled her. Patty took a lot of pride in her family's high economic standing.

"Tramp?" Jane sneered loudly. "You're not a tramp. You're a pro! You take care of every guy on varsity, and you've got enough endurance left for the junior varsity!"

Patty rose up on the balls of her feet and glared down on her. "Why you little piece of waste! You call me a pro when you practically publish what you do in bed!"

"Girls—" Kirk said.

Out the corner of her eye, Jane saw that Dr. Palmer and Mr. Pan were already on the move toward them. She would have to pull out all the stops. "How much did Kirk pay you?" she shouted. "Did you give him his money's worth?" She shoved Kirk in the chest. "Come on, what did she charge you?"

Kirk's eyes narrowed. From experience, she knew how he hated anyone shoving him. "I wouldn't pay that girl for nothing."

Patty glared at him. "And what's that supposed to mean, monkey brain?"

Kirk sucked in a breath. He also disliked people making references to his lack of intelligence. "What's what? You talk so sweet, but inside you're nothing but trash. Trying to fool me with that phony diary page. No damn way you're going to fool me!"

The three of them were practically nose to nose, and the boat's pitching forced them even closer. So far so good, Jane thought, but she needed more hostility from them, and she needed it quickly. Alice's dad had only a half-dozen steps to take before he'd be close enough to pull them apart.

Fortunately, she had an unlooked-for ally.

"Stop it!" Dr. Palmer hollered, stepping over a coil of rope. "There'll be no swearing as long as I'm captain of this ship!"

"Let them be," Mr. Pan said, grabbing Dr. Palmer from behind, slowing him down. "Let them work out their hatred."

Dr. Palmer whirled, flailing his chubby hands. "Let go of me! I'll have you put below!"

"Fighting is natural," Mr. Pan told him.

The adult distraction along with a particularly large and unbalancing swell gave Jane the opportunity to slip her hand through Patty's arm and pinch Kirk's crotch. Jane supposed there wasn't a guy on the planet who would have liked *that*. Kirk thought Patty had done it.

"Bitch!" he swore, pushing Patty into her.

Patty slapped him across the face. "Jackass!"

Jane wrestled between them, grabbing them both near the belt, clutching their flesh as well as their clothes, making it look—for the benefit of her audience—as if Kirk and Patty were wrestling with her. "Leave me alone!" she screamed. "You're hurting me!"

Kirk tried to pull away, giving her a slight push. Patty slashed out with a fist that caught Jane square on the skull.

Jane didn't have to fake it. The blow was enough. The gunwale of the boat was suddenly above her. Sky and water switched positions as her vision whirled.

Good-bye.

"It's healthy," Mr. Pan said.

Those were the last words she heard. A wave hit her with a hard slap. Then it was cold and dark.

CHAPTER VIII

IN ALL HER PLANNING, JANE HAD NEVER CONSIDERED THAT she would barely be able to see while only a few feet beneath the surface. Because she was so used to diving with a mask on, she had forgotten how poor visibility was with salt water in your eyes. Her backward plunge into the water had not helped matters.

Where am I?

The hull of the boat loomed off to her left like a blurred white whale. She couldn't even see the rudder. Shadows of bubbles rose in the direction of her feet. Great, she was upside down. Her sinuses felt as if they were bursting from the pressure of expanding ice; she had taken a lot of water up the nose. The night before, snug inside her full wet suit, the ocean had felt thirty degrees warmer.

Fortunately, she didn't panic; she didn't have time. *Wild Wind* was crawling at a snail's pace, but even so, the ship would be past her within seconds unless she hooked on somewhere. It had been her original intention to immediately swim to where she had attached the scuba equipment. Now that would have to wait until she got her bearings.

Jane twisted around, stroking downward, her sweat-

87

er bunching up on her arms, soaked and heavy. The momentum of her clumsy dive had carried her approximately fifteen feet from the ship. Quickly, she closed the distance, feeling forward with her hands. Her search was not entirely haphazard. When they were about to set off, Dr. Palmer had wrestled with a boarding ladder, but he never had been able to pull it up all the way. It lay at about midship.

A glint of metal caught her attention, above and off to her left. That had to be it. Kicking hard, she thrust out her arms. Something hard cracked her knuckles. She closed her fingers around it and felt the yank go through the length of her body. She was being towed.

Jane didn't remember having taken a breath before hitting the water, but she must have grabbed a good one; her lungs were not complaining in the least. But then, she had only been under about fifteen seconds. Yet already they must be waiting for her to break surface. Now that she knew where she was, it was time to jump ship altogether.

Blinking, her eyes adjusting somewhat to the dimness and the salt water, she shoved off the ladder with her legs and again swam downward, pulling slightly to her right, following the curve of the hull, seeing the rudder for the first time. However, as rapidly as the visibility had begun to improve, it started to fail. By going under the boat, she was slipping into its shadow, losing what feeble light the sky far above had to offer.

It's not here! It must have fallen off!

She couldn't see the equipment. Worse, far worse, she suddenly realized she had not checked to see if Dr. Palmer had been running the engine. He'd had the sails up, but the wind had been dismal. It was possible—at the moment, it seemed likely—that he had resorted to the engine for a little extra boost. If she continued to float in her present position, her face might be kissing a triad of hungry propellers any second.

Jane strained her eyes through the salty gloom. And damn her stupid brilliance if there wasn't a whirlwind of turbulence toward the rear of the ship. At least she thought there might be. Suddenly she couldn't be sure of anything.

She began to panic.

I've got to get out of here!

She no longer knew which way was up.

What saved her, for the moment, was her paralysis. By drifting and doing nothing, she had naturally begun to bobble toward the surface, right into the rudder. A black ball bumped her shoulder. Instinctively, she grabbed it, putting herself once again under tow.

She'd found the scuba gear.

A few seconds of anxiety could consume a lot of oxygen. In an instant she went from the terror of being shredded to the nightmare of drowning. A thick band began to tighten around her chest. Relying solely on touch for guidance, she fumbled for the valve to the air tank, a silent wail in her head oscillating rapidly into a full-throated shriek.

I'm dying. I'm dying. I'm dying.

Many painful heartbeats later, she found the valve right where it was supposed to be—at the top of the tank. Giving it a frantic clockwise twist, she sent a stream of ghostly bubbles piling into her face. Clawing toward their source, she thrust the mouthpiece into her mouth and created a watertight seal by biting down hard enough to crack a fossilized nut with her teeth.

A little air sure could make life a lot easier.

For a full minute Jane breathed gratefully, strength and confidence pouring back into her limbs. When she was fully sated, she glanced around—the bottled air had even improved her eyesight—and noticed to her amazement that the turbulence at the rear of the boat was not being caused by propellers, but by kicking legs and arms.

They're looking for me. Isn't that nice.

It also made sense they were searching for her in the wrong place. They couldn't know she had used the boat to tow her away from where she entered the water. Nevertheless, she was still too close for safety. Holding the mouthpiece securely in place with one hand, she unhooked her equipment and the clamp that had held it in place, and pushed off lightly with her feet. She began to sink almost immediately.

Jane could not be sure of the precise depth of the water, but she had figured it must be close to fifty feet. Although she was going down more swiftly than she would have under ordinary circumstances, by repeatedly popping her ears, she kept the pressure from building inside her head. It was while coming back to the surface that you had to be careful to take your time.

The light faded steadily and soon vanished altogether, leaving her drifting in a freezing void without a single visual reference. Yet her panic did not return. Indeed, she began to experience a strange euphoria. As far as the world was concerned, she no longer existed; and the majority of her senses would have agreed with the world. More than at any other time in her life, she found it easy to pretend that she was more than flesh and blood, that she had died and survived to think about it.

When her feet finally did touch the ocean floor, she could hardly feel it. Her toes were completely numb, and her lower legs would be along soon to join them The temperature was at least fifteen degrees lower than that at the surface. She remembered Sharon's warning about cramping. It was time for phase two.

Jane flicked on the waterproof flashlight she had taped to the side of the tanks, pointing it into the sand. The light came out a sober red; she had colored the glass the night before, worried that those up above might be able to spot her. Her concern had been unnecessary; the light appeared to penetrate no more than an arm's length in any direction before encountering an impenetrable wall of pure darkness.

The next step was to put on her face mask and clear it. Looking surfaceward, holding the mask firmly against her forehead with both hands, she exhaled steadily through her nose. The air entering the face plate began to occupy the upper portion of the mask, forcing the water out the bottom. She could actually see the water level dropping before her blurred vision as she continued to exhale.

My God, look at them all!

To her immense surprise, she could suddenly see the silver outline of the surface, the shadowed hull of *Wild Wind*, and the faint motion of a dozen searching swimmers. But she wasn't concerned her classmates would see her. She understood well the principle of the one-way mirror. They were visible to her because they were in a relatively well lit area. She would be invisible to them because she was in a darker region.

As long as they stay on the surface.

Other people besides Alice had brought scuba equipment aboard. If Sharon had been unable to isolate Alice and explain the situation, Alice could possibly be preparing to dive down into the depths. Again Jane cautioned herself to hurry, sliding out of the sweater and into the rest of the wet suit, pulling on her fins, and fitting the air-tank harness over her shoulders. Life quickly returned to her icy skin. Her weight belt and flotation device went on next. Finally, she strapped a phosphorescent compass over her right wrist; she already wore a diver's watch on her left wrist. Turning off her light, she oriented herself in a northern direction and set off at a respectable clip. Dark sand swept beneath her as she left *Wild Wind* and Wilcox High's finest behind.

On her back was a 71.2-cubic-foot, 2250-psi tank. From experience, she knew the air would last approximately forty minutes at this depth, longer if she moved closer to the surface. It was her plan to consume half her air before resurfacing, saving the remainder for when she hit the beach; should she happen to come up where there were people, she wanted to have the option of moving underwater to another locale. She had excellent endurance. In twenty minutes, she would be able to put a mile between her and the boat.

After the excitement of provoking Kirk and Patty and the fright of not being able to reach the equipment, the long swim proved somewhat anticlimactic. Her euphoria started to fade. In this area, the ocean floor was remarkably featureless, with few plants and even fewer fish. The sand slipped beneath her with almost hypnotic sameness. But at one point the surface overhead began to change from silver to blue. The sun had topped the horizon.

After swimming for twenty minutes, she partially inflated her flotation device and began to curve upward in a long sweeping arc, again carefully popping her ears. By now she was begining to feel the first signs of fatigue. Her left hamstring had tightened the night before while she was planting the equipment, and the same tightness had now returned. It would be good to breath real air again.

Popping into daylight, she found herself at the exact top of a huge swell. A brief glance around was enough to locate *Wild Wind*.

"Woh!" She laughed aloud. It looked so tiny, so far away. Another boat of about half the size appeared to be closing on it; no doubt to render assistance in locating the body.

Good luck, fellas.

Since she had swum parallel to the shore, she had gained no ground on it; the beach was still a mile away. However, the hardest part was over. From now on she would be able to see exactly where she was going. She began to dog paddle lazily toward land.

The early hour favored her. Except for a stray jogger far south, there was no one on the beach. For this she was grateful. Her left leg had begun to stiffen painfully, and even treading water with the help of her fins and flotation ballon hurt. She hung off shore for a break in the swells, and when it finally came, she put the remainder of her energy into a mad dash for the sand. But when she reached it, and had slipped off her fins, she had difficulty getting to her feet and had to lie panting for several minutes on the ground.

"You did it, baby," she whispered. "You're incredible."

Her celebration would have to wait. If she was spotted now and a reasonable description was passed on to the police, she could be in serious trouble. That was unlikely, however, and she had anticipated her present fatigue and had parked her car nearby so she could make a quick getaway. She hoped the blasted carburetor would get her to Sharon's cabin in the hills. The police would head to Jane's house first, looking for her parents. Thank God her mom and dad were completely isolated in the mountains. She planned on spending the entire weekend at Sharon's place.

And then she would show up at school on Monday as if nothing had happened. She could hardly wait.

Jane pulled off her equipment, bundled it into an easy-to-carry pile, and hiked up to the road. It turned out she had hit the beach only a couple of blocks from her car. Walking the deserted sidewalks past the sleeping houses, she felt like whistling. It wouldn't surprise her one bit if Kirk and Patty had already been arrested.

"Leave me alone! You're hurting me!"

Instead of whistling, Jane laughed.

Her car, and the key taped to the bottom of the engine, were where she had left them, in an alley behind a McDonald's. Stowing the gear in the trunk, she got behind the wheel, mumbled a silent prayer, and turned the ignition. To her immense relief, the car started without a hitch, and she was on her way.

Before she could get out of town, however, Jane realized she had made the same mistake that had been the death of villains and heroes throughout modern history. She had forgotten to make sure she had enough gas. The needle lay between the quarter mark and the big *E*. Climbing the road to the cabin would use a lot of fuel, especially with her out-of-tune engine. But stopping for gas would be risky if her picture was being flashed on local TV stations. Then again, she didn't have any money. For a minute she debated swinging by her house. Her dad kept a couple of gallons of gas in the garage for his lawn mower.

Yet, in the end, she decided against it. Even if she had to walk part of the way to the cabin, it would be better to play it safe.

The big *E* caught up with her five minutes too soon. About two miles from her destination, on a crummy collection of asphalt that passed for a road, the Toyota spurted and died, leaving her with just enough momentum to roll off to the side. The latter move wasn't crucial. Sharon's parents had built their cabin in a rather isolated area of the hills. There wasn't another place around for miles. Except for Sharon, chances were no one would be coming up the road in the next two days.

Jane parked and got out. The past summer had been particularly hot and dry. The local terrain was more brown than green. Standing there in her shorts, Jane could feel the warmth of the sun on her tired legs. Although she was very much aware of her isolation, she worried about abandoning her rented equipment in the trunk of the car. The catch on the lock was broken, and if someone happened by he could give it a solid yank and be off with a thousand bucks' worth of gear that she'd have to pay for. She couldn't very well go reporting such a theft to the police.

I'll carry it. I'll have plenty of time to rest when I get there.

Jane discovered another minor hole in her planning as she trudged up the rough road with the tank and wet suit slung over her shoulder. She had forgotten about shoes, making her choice of courses lousy: she could either walk on the asphalt—which was already beginning to cook—or she could stay on the shoulder in the dirt with all its nasty prickly thorns. She ended up alternating from one to the other, and as a result, both burned and bloodied the soles of her feet.

It took her over an hour to cover the last two miles.

The cabin was open frame, two stories of lacquered redwood, set on the side of a steep hill. A row of thick upright logs supported the rear. Jane understood that Sharon's parents had situated the structure in such a precarious position for the sake of the view; nevertheless, she would have hated to be inside in the event of an earthquake. The cabin had a front door, but the back door was no way out; it led onto a small porch situated high above the ground.

Sharon's parents kept a key to the cabin hidden under a stone behind a tree about fifty yards from the porch. Fetching it, Jane unlocked the front door and stumbled inside where she collapsed in a chair in the kitchen.

The freezer better be stocked like Sharon promised.

Jane rested a few minutes before drinking about half a gallon of water. It tasted wonderful, and she was thinking of having more when she remembered the day's big story. She ran into the living room and turned on the radio and TV.

Hey, I'm dead. What are all these cartoons?

A half hour of listening and watching brought her

not a word about her untimely end. When she thought about it realistically, she supposed she didn't rate a special bulletin. But the news would be on later, and she hoped she'd be at "the top of the hour."

She felt guilty when she saw how she had dumped her messy gear on the spotless floor. There was sand all over the tank and wet suit. Remembering that the only finished bathroom was upstairs off the master bedroom, she gathered together the stuff and crawled up the steps, every muscle in her body aching.

I'll take a hot shower and clean the equipment at the same time.

Jane didn't quite make it. She deposited the gear in the bathtub and went back into the bedroom for a moment. Then she sat on the bed to take a splinter out of her foot. But she couldn't find it—she might even have had the wrong foot, she was so groggy with exhaustion—and she decided to lie back for a second before looking further. Putting her head down did it. She went out like a light.

It was dark when she awoke. Her sleep had been deep and dreamless. Glancing down, she realized she hadn't moved the whole time; her bare legs were still dangling over the side of the bed. The window above the chest of drawers had been left open. Goose pimples covered her exposed flesh. A deep silence pervaded the whole hilltop. She could hear her heart slowly pounding.

A glance at her watch made her sit up with a start. The news would begin in two minutes! This she couldn't miss. Bouncing off the bed, she hurried downstairs, flipped on the TV, and huddled in the corner of the couch. As the pretty redheaded anchorwoman came on the screen, Jane began to bite her nails through a wide grin.

Her grin did not last.

"Hello, I'm Kathy Morrison. Welcome to News at Seven on KNIT. Our top story tonight: tragedy strikes a school boating trip. This morning at dawn, aboard the sailing ship *Wild Wind,* a series of arguments and accidents led to the death of two teenagers: seventeen-year-old Jane Retton and eighteen-year-old Kirk Donner."

Pictures of Kirk and herself appeared beside Ms. Morrison's head. Jane blinked, not understanding. The lady continued.

"The outing was to be a weekend of pleasure. A prominent local dentist, Dr. Palmer, had rented the boat and invited approximately five dozen of his daughter's classmates to sail out to the Santa Barbara Islands. Problems began when Jane Retton got into an argument with two other teens: Patty Brane, head cheerleader of Wilcox High, and Kirk Donner, boyfriend of Jane Retton. The cause of the argument is not clear at this time, but during the course of it, Jane Retton either fell or was pushed overboard. She did not resurface, and police are speculating that she may have struck her head on the hull of the boat while going into the sea. Approximately thirty minutes later, while efforts were being made in the water by a number of students to locate Miss Retton, Kirk Donner drowned. Donner was the first to begin diving and had continued to dive repeatedly even when it became apparent that Jane wouldn't be found alive. Since he was close to Jane Retton, the police feel he must have driven himself past the point of exhaustion and cramped. His body was discovered floating face down not far from the ship. Resuscitation efforts proved unsuccessful. . . ."

A mistake, there must be a mistake.

Denial and grief cracked through Jane's soul. Kirk could have swum all the way to the islands without cramping. It was simply impossible that he had drowned. No, this lady had her facts jumbled; she always did have a tendency to exaggerate.

It's me, only me, who drowned! Damn you, shut up!

At the same time, a part of her knew with absolute surety that Kirk was dead and that she was responsible.

Ignoring the TV, the follow-up interviews with lieutenants and lifeguards, she slowly crossed the room to the telephone, a lifeless wraith in a nightmare she had dreamed up for her own amusement. She would call Alice. Dr. Palmer would come and get her. The police would question her. Maybe she would make bail, maybe not. She didn't care. Suddenly she didn't care about anything except how she had blamed Kirk for her humiliation when she had known in her heart that he'd had almost nothing to do with it.

But the phone was dead.

The TV flickered off. The lights went out.

CHAPTER IX

In the Room

"WHEN JANE WENT OVERBOARD AND DIDN'T COME UP, THE whole boat freaked out," Alice said.

"Did you know at that time about Jane's plan?" Fisher asked.

"No. I wish Sharon had told me sooner. I could have killed her. Afterward, she said there was too much commotion, that she couldn't get me alone, which I suppose was true. Right away, I went into the water with a bunch of other people."

"Did Kirk dive in?"

"Yeah. When Jane didn't come up after a few seconds, he didn't even wait to take off his shirt. He was frantic to find her. We all were."

"Go on."

Alice gestured helplessly. "It was awful. We kept looking and there was nothing. You know, even when people drown, they usually float to the surface. We didn't know what to do. Finally, my dad had me get into my scuba equipment and go to the bottom."

"Did you see any sign of Jane's equipment down there?"

"No, nothing. But at that depth, I didn't make a real thorough check."

"Why not?"

Alice's lip quivered. "If I found her on the floor, I knew I'd just be finding her body."

"And all this time, Kirk was in the water?"

"Yes. He stayed in the whole time. He had a snorkel and face mask."

"How did he drown?"

Alice had been expecting the question. "I think he got the bends. He was going down too deep, coming up too quickly. The lifeguard who boarded *Wild Wind* after the patrol boat came up alongside us said that was unlikely, but I don't think he knew what he was talking about. Unequipped pearl divers in the South Pacific get the bends all the time the same way."

"Kirk was a strong swimmer?"

"He sure was. He was taking two-minute dives. I'm not kidding."

"Did you have an eye on him the whole time?"

Alice paused. "Not the whole time."

Fisher frowned. "I still don't see how he could have drowned, a kid like that who had grown up beside the ocean."

"Have you ever had the bends?"

"No. Have you?"

She nodded. "Once. You get nitrogen bubbles in your blood. You feel as if you're having convulsions. If the bends hit him while he was under, I don't know what he could have done."

"Kirk was actually diving to the ocean floor?"

"Almost, yeah."

"Were you letting him breathe from your tank?"

The question surprised her. "What? No. Why would I do that? We weren't that close together."

"But that is something divers sometimes do? They share air?"

101

Alice appeared doubtful. "When there's an emergency, yeah."

"Was anyone else in scuba equipment besides you?"

"No."

"Didn't anyone else dive?"

"Yes. But my father only wanted me to go to the bottom."

"Why just you?"

"I'm not sure. He knows how experienced I am. He might have been afraid of a current in the area. He probably thought that's what had sucked Jane under."

"And yet he let you risk your life? His own daughter?"

"My father trusts me." She lowered her head, rubbed at her mouth.

"You wanted to add something?"

"No. Well, just that currents like that are rare."

Everything Alice had said made sense. It would completely rewrite the afternoon's report on Kirk Donner's drowning. Yet Fisher felt he was missing something vital, something that was staring him right in the face. "When did Sharon tell you the truth?" he asked.

"Not until we were back on shore."

"Why didn't you go straight to the police?"

"I didn't want to be the one to turn Jane in."

"But weren't you furious at her?"

"I was—upset. I was relieved that she was alive. But I felt so bad about Kirk. Sharon was throwing a fit."

"She blamed Jane?"

"Totally. I've never seen her so angry."

"Why didn't Sharon tell the police the truth?"

"I'm not sure. I think she wanted to talk to Jane first."

"I'm confused here. You both knew where Jane was. Why didn't you drive up to the cabin?"

Alice shook her head. "That was the last thing I wanted to do. I didn't want to be the one who broke it to Jane about Kirk. Sharon's known her longer, anyway. She said she was going up."

"And that was the last you saw of Sharon?"

"Yes."

"What did you do then?"

"I went home."

"About what time was this?"

"Midafternoon."

"You stayed home all day? Till tonight when you asked your father to bring you down here to the station?"

"Yes."

"What did you do all day?"

"I rested." Alice hesitated. "I did try to call Jane at the cabin, but only after I didn't hear from Sharon."

"Did you speak to her?"

"No. The call wouldn't go through. I don't know why."

"Did you ask the operator for help?"

"No. I've never asked the operator for help."

"Didn't you begin to worry when neither Sharon nor Jane called you?"

"I started to worry, yeah, but not that they were dead."

"Did you become friends with Sharon after you met Jane?"

"Yes."

"Did you like Sharon?"

"Sure."

"Did she like Kirk?"

"Why do you ask?"

"I never know what might be important. Did she like him? In a romantic way?"

Alice considered a long time. "Maybe."

Fisher glanced at the clock. Almost three in the morning. The father wouldn't wait forever. Fisher couldn't afford to handle Alice gently any longer. They were getting down to the nitty-gritty. Shocking her might help jar her memory. "When Sharon left you, was she mad enough to kill?"

"Sharon couldn't have killed a fly."

"Are you sure? She had the motivation. Jane was indirectly responsible for Kirk's death. No one knew that better than Sharon."

Alice shook her head. "That's such a weird idea."

Fisher leaned forward. "No, it's not. Only two people in the world knew Jane was still alive: you and Sharon."

Alice stared at him with her big eyes opened wide. "I didn't kill her," she whispered.

Fisher sharpened his voice. "Who did?"

"I don't know."

"Why couldn't it have been Sharon?"

A tear welled up in the corner of her eye. "She wouldn't have done it. She was a good person."

"But what about Jane? She was a good person, too. Why did you say she committed suicide?"

"I didn't say that!" Alice said, hurt by his change in tone.

"Yes, you did. You said it right at the start."

She looked to the side, breathing heavily. "No, I said I thought *maybe* she had killed herself."

"Why would you think that? How would you know?"

"I don't know!"

"Then why did you say it?"

"There were radios and TVs at the cabin. Jane must have heard about Kirk." Alice wiped at her face with her shaking hand. "She must have felt terrible."

"Terrible enough to set the place on fire and put herself to the worst death imaginable? And you say my ideas are weird? Come on, Alice, where's Sharon?"

Alice burst out crying. "I don't know!"

CHAPTER X

Jane had never been afraid of the dark, not even as a little girl. Whereas most children felt that *something* could get them when the lights were off, Jane had always felt she could hide from the same *something* if given enough shadows. When the lights failed at the cabin, she initially felt not even a twinge of personal danger. Kirk, or rather the absence of Kirk, had colored her universe so black that the external darkness might even have been welcome. Except for one thing.

The phone was also out.

Do phones fail with the power?

It had been dead before the lights went out.

A large sliding glass door led onto the back porch. Far away, the lights of the city twinkled beside the flat expanse of the ocean, and hanging above—a crescent moon, spreading its cool sheen through the drapes on the glass door as they parted slightly with the night-time breeze. Jane stepped to the door and grasped the handle. She didn't remember having opened it.

Sharon was supposed to be here. . . .

Jane moved out onto the porch, staying away from the railing, searching without success for the fuse box. Hazarding a glance downward, she couldn't even locate the base of the poles that supported the house above the steep dry valley. They seemed to disappear into the air rather than into the ground. It was a long way to the bottom.

She decided the main electrical cables must have been wired through the garage. Stepping back inside, closing the door at her back, she went into the kitchen. Away from the window, the darkness was almost as thick as it had been on the ocean floor. She had to feel her way forward.

The door that led from the kitchen to the garage wouldn't open. The knob turned freely; the door simply wouldn't budge. Jane didn't fight it long. She could circle around outside. And if the power line really had gone down, the fuse box wasn't going to help her anyway.

The front door opened handily. The instant before she went outside, however, she paused, not knowing why. No flicker of motion had caught the corner of her eye. No faint creaking had reached her ears. Yet she stood for a long time, watching, listening, wondering again how the only boy who had ever kissed her could this very moment be lying dead in the city morgue.

Did I love him? Or did I love the idea that he might love me?

Jane put one foot on the front porch.

A gun went off. The window beside her shattered into a thousand pieces. Jane dived back into the house and slammed the door shut with her foot.

"Jesus," she whispered, lying face down on the kitchen floor, her heart hammering in her chest, splinters of glass grinding beneath her sweaty palms. They were trying to kill her!

Yes, but who are "they"?

She'd worry about that later. Right now she had to get out of the cabin. That should be easy enough. All she had to do was strap a set of wings on her back and jump off the back porch and glide down to the city. Sure, Jumpin' Jane. Damn this house! It must be the only one she had visited in her entire life that didn't have a back door you could escape through.

It occurred to her she couldn't hear anyone approaching. Were they holding back for fear she was armed? If so, they would not stay put long without return fire.

The shot had sounded strange, muffled as though a pillow had been wrapped around the gun barrel to prevent the noise from spreading to the rest of the hills. Obviously this whole affair was one they didn't want anyone to know about.

Keeping her head down, Jane crawled in the direction of the stairs. Several splinters of glass remained lodged in her hands, causing warm blood to ooze from between her fingers, leaving splotches on the clean carpet, splotches she could readily imagine in the dark even though she couldn't see them very clearly. The cuts and blood had a more hideous effect on her than merely slowing her down. They reminded her all too vividly that she had a body and that without that body, she had nothing. The logic was terribly simple, terribly obtuse, and also, at the moment, terribly important to her. She couldn't die. If she died, she wouldn't be able to flip back to page one of her diary and rework the story.

The stairs led her back up to the master bedroom. Once in the room she wondered what the hell she was doing there. Then it struck her. Perhaps her subconscious had been trying to push her in the right direction. Sharon's parents had mildly paranoid dispositions. Chances were they kept a gun beside their bed.

Jane ventured into a crouched position. The window facing the road exploded with a loud bang. Jane got down on her hands and knees. More glass dug into her palms. More blood stained the carpet.

Jane discovered she was crying. That was fine, she decided, as long as she didn't freeze into a whimpering ball. With tears streaming over her cheeks, keeping her head down, she quickly went through the drawers in the nightstands on either side of the bed, then searched under the bed, through the closet. Nothing, no gun and yet Mr. Less took target practice at least once a month.

Then she checked beneath the pillows.

Major paranoia.

A high-caliber snub-nosed six-chamber revolver lay under the left pillow, fully loaded. Her relief lasted a total of five seconds. What was she supposed to shoot at? She couldn't see them, even know if *them* was one, two, or three. She seriously doubted if she fired a single shot into the air they would get scared and run away. Also, she didn't want to volunteer that she had a weapon.

Jane crawled out of the room and stood up in the hallway. Here there were no windows and she paused to collect her wits. The fact that there was only one entrance could work to her advantage, she realized. Her position was easily defensible. They couldn't come through the garage without making a lot of noise. All she had to do was tuck herself into a dark corner and guard the front door, let them make the first move.

No reason I couldn't just stay put till dawn.

Jane had settled herself halfway down the stairway and had been sitting there for approximately fifteen minutes when she heard footsteps. The sound sent shivers from her toes to her head. They must be confident she was defenseless. They were coming rapidly, making no attempt at secrecy.

She listened closer, and her escalating tension suddenly leveled off. There was only one pair of feet out there. A wave of unexpected courage flooded through her body. The odds would be even, maybe even in her favor. Moving swiftly but silently, she hurried down the remaining stairs. As she passed the fireplace, the poker caught her eye, and she picked it up as much for psychological as for tactical reasons. Its steel weight felt good in her clenched fingers. Switching the revolver to her left hand, she took up a position behind the closed front door.

The steps grew louder and louder. Jane sucked in a breath, held it. A hand touched the front door, slowly turned the handle.

Use the gun! Use the gun! Use the gun!

Even before the door began to open, Jane realized she would be unable to pull the trigger. She had read a thousand books where the heroine had been saved in the end by a timely shot placed between the villain's eyes. But those shots had been fired by girls who could put holes in people on page twenty-six and make out with their boyfriends on page forty-two and not even mess up their hair in between. It struck her then that perhaps she had spent too much of her life trying to imitate people who didn't exist.

If only I were imagining this.

The door began to open. Jane raised the poker. The silhouette of a head pushed inside. Jane brought down the poker.

The blow caught the person on the left temple, near the ear. A faint cry escaped her lips—it was a girl, God—before she toppled forward onto the floor. Dropping the poker and stuffing the revolver inside her belt, Jane grabbed the girl and pulled her all the way inside, then quickly closed the door.

She ain't going anywhere.

Even in the dismal light, Jane could see a puddle of dark fluid gathering beside the girl's head. Feeling a combination of relief and pride, guilt and self-loathing, she took hold of her conquest by the arms and dragged her into the living room where the moonlight was brightest.

"No!" Jane cried involuntarily a moment later, letting go of the body, cringing in horror.

It was her best friend, Sharon.

She was trying to kill me!

A new noise, far worse than bullets and footsteps, told her just how wrong she was.

The ruined window beside the front door exploded again. A bottle splattered across the kitchen carpet as a half gallon of liquid fire spilled out and instantly began to devour anything that would burn. Jane watched in absolute horror as the flames slithered up the wallpaper to the curtains, transforming them into a sheet of raging orange death. Within seconds, before she could budge an inch, both the way to the front door and the path to the garage door became impassable. The possibility of extinguishing the fire with a sheet or something went straight to zero.

Jane fell to her knees, rolled her old friend over, and shook her violently. "Sharon, wake up! Sharon, we have to go! Sharon!"

Sharon's head bobbled loosely from side to side. Jane left her for a moment and dashed to the sliding glass door that led to the porch. A check outside told her that, no, the drop to the ground had not decreased in the last ten minutes. Also, for the first time, she noticed the rocks far below, their hard edges sharp in the clear moonlight. Yet the poles that supported the balcony offered probably their only possibility of escape. If they could get over the railing without falling, they might be able to wrap their arms and legs around the poles and slowly work their way down. It had come down to hard choices, and Jane decided she'd rather break her neck than get fried.

Back inside, the air was rapidly becoming unbreathable. The flames had consumed the kitchen and were reaching along the floor for the living room sofa. Jane went down on her knees once more and cradled Sharon's head in her hands. The cut from the blow continued to bleed, and Jane cursed herself again and again for having been so dense. Sharon had said she would come. Her tardiness could easily be explained by the fact that her driver's license had been revoked. Chances were she had ridden her bike to the cabin, or at least to the base of the final hill. From all the footsteps Jane had heard, she guessed Sharon must have walked the last leg. Walked in as innocent as a lamb going to its slaughter.

A pity she hadn't been warned away by the shots. But they had been—when? Twenty minutes ago? Sharon must have been too far away to hear them.

"Sharon, please hear me! Wake up! We can't stay!"

It was no use. Sharon didn't even stir. Bending under the weight of a crushing hopelessness, Jane buried her face in Sharon's hair, choking on the smoke, weeping in her misery.

What can I do? I can't do anything.

A moment later Jane had an idea. The stairs and the upper portion of the house had yet to be touched by the flames. If she could get Sharon into the master bedroom and push her out the window, at least Sharon would stand a chance. Even though the bedroom was on the second story, the drop from its window had to be half the length of the drop off the balcony. And maybe there wouldn't be any rocks where Sharon landed.

Yet as quick as the possibility formed in her mind, fear and logic rose up to stomp it down.

If I slide down the poles now, right now, whoever has the gun won't see me. I can escape through the gorge. I'll make it. But if I go upstairs, I might get trapped. I might die. I probably will die, and Sharon's probably going to die anyway.

She let go of Sharon, took a step toward the balcony. But before she could walk three feet, she doubled up as if she had been belted in the stomach; and it was not smoke alone that made her choke, but a sickening sense of loss. Turning and seeing her childhood friend lying helpless on the floor, the fire moving closer and closer, she knew in her heart that if she left, she would be as guilty of murder as the madman outside.

I was the one who started all this.

Finally Jane came to a firm decision, and it gave her strength. She actually *carried* Sharon up the stairs. When she had come down a few minutes earlier, she had automatically closed the bedroom door behind her; the room was therefore relatively free of smoke. After going inside and shutting the door, Jane deposited Sharon on the bed and went to the shattered window, hoping he or she with the itchy trigger finger had gone.

No such luck.

With a bang, the window on her right suddenly splintered, toppling to the floor. Falling to the carpet, Jane crawled to the bed, grabbed hold of Sharon's feet, then dragged her into the bathroom and dumped her in the tub on top of the scuba equipment. There Jane was able to stand again; the bathroom window was tiny, but it faced east, off the side of the house, and theoretically should not be visible to the gunman.

Unfortunately, it was stuck, stuck hard. Frantic, Jane looked around for something to break it with. The best she could come up with was a jar of cold cream, but that broke in her hands the moment she pounded on the thick glass.

We're going to die, and all because Mr. and Mrs. Less keep a gun in their bedroom, but not a scale in their bathroom.

Jane did not want to die alone. For the time being, the plumbing still worked; she flooded Sharon's face with a stream of cold water. Her friend finally began to show signs of life, wincing beneath the shower. Jane crouched beside her, getting wet.

"Sharon, it's Jane. Wake up, sleepyhead."

Sharon's glazed eyes half opened. "Jane?"

Jane glanced out through the bathroom door. The cracks around the bedroom door glowed an ugly red. The fire had followed them up the stairs. Sharon had slept a couple of minutes too long. The temperature was rising rapidly. "It's me," Jane said, turning back to her friend. "How do you feel?"

Sharon groaned, turning her head painfully. "I'm cold. Why is it raining?"

Jane turned off the shower, and the water vanished down the drain, tinged red with Sharon's blood. Jane stroked her friend's hand gently. "Is that better?"

Sharon grimaced. "I feel funny. I fell, I think."

"Just lie still. You'll feel better soon." The bedroom door started to blacken as a gray vapor poured off the walls. "Very soon," Jane said, sweat dripping from every pore in her body.

Sharon's eyes wandered dreamily about. "Am I in the bathtub?"

"Yes."

Sharon nodded slightly. "I helped my daddy put it in when I was a little girl."

Jane could feel her tears again. "I know you did."

Sharon's eyelids fell shut, and her words were slurred. "I was my daddy's—favorite girl."

Jane leaned over and kissed her on the forehead. "You're my favorite, too."

Sharon smiled faintly. "I love—"

She didn't finish, lapsing back into unconsciousness.

Maybe we'll talk again in a few minutes. If I don't end up in hell.

The bedroom door collapsed. A geyser of smoke and fire poured in, sending forth a blast of superheated air that pushed Jane to the edge of a blackout. The fine hairs on her bare arms crackled and fizzled. Blood beaded on her suddenly parched lips. Inhaling became out of the question. Turning the valve on the scuba tank, Jane held the mouthpiece to Sharon's lips, holding her own breath. She was wasting her time. You had to bite down on the mouthpiece for it to work, and you had to be awake to do that. It didn't matter, anyway. After shaking Sharon, slapping her face, pinching her heel, Jane came to the realization—and it brought her a small measure of comfort—that Sharon was already beyond all pain. Even when the flames came dancing in, she would remain asleep.

Jane took the air for herself. She knew she would be dead before she could finish the tank.

It's done now. It's over.

Then she had an idea, a really incredible idea.

As the fire jumped onto the king-size bed, transforming it into a playpen for devils, Jane lifted Sharon out of the tub and turned the shower back on.

CHAPTER XI

FISHER DECIDED HE HAD PUSHED ALICE TOO FAR TOO QUICK-
ly. His demand that she tell him Sharon's whereabouts had been the straw that had broken the camel's
back. A couple of minutes had passed and she was still
crying, her bowed head partly hidden behind her
beautiful black hair.

"Would you like another soda?" he asked finally.

She sniffed. "No."

"Can we talk some more?"

She glanced up, rubbing her eyes. Even without
makeup, they were striking. "I don't have anything
else to say."

"I'm grateful for what you have told me." He toyed
with his empty Coke can, repressing the urge to crush
it. He couldn't remember having ever felt so frus-
trated. He supposed any homicide investigator would
have gone nuts having to label a case like this a suicide
after having listened to a testimonial on the indomitable spirit of the victim.

How could you have let yourself die, Jane?

If only Sharon would call.

"Can I go home now?" Alice asked.

"Of course. But before you do, please do me a favor

and wait just a few minutes more." He stood. "I need to check something with my partner."

"Okay."

Fisher couldn't immediately locate Officer Rick. While looking, he decided to have a quick peek in the room where they had been holding Patty Brane. To his surprise, she hadn't left yet. Sitting alone, she smiled when she saw it was he.

"Hi, handsome, working late?"

He stepped inside, closing the door behind him. "Where're your parents, your lawyer?"

Patty shrugged, tugging on a curl of her bleached hair. She had to be as tired as he was; nevertheless, her eyes raked him over good. Alice had been right about one thing; this girl was always ready for action. "They went to have a *private* conference. They think I'm too young to listen in." She smiled slyly. "But I'm not that young, you know."

The room had two doors, opposite each other. The parents and lawyer must be standing right outside in the other hall. He pulled up a chair beside her. He could get in trouble if he was caught, personal rights and all that. He would have to talk fast. "Could you and I have a little chat, strictly off the record?" he asked.

"I don't think I should, not here at least. But if you wanted to come by my place, say, Monday afternoon, when my parents are out."

"Patty, I'm serious."

"So am I." She straightened his tie. "Who takes care of you, anyway?"

He tactfully took away her hand. Yeah, he could get in hot water all right. "I want to make you an offer.

118

I've just had a long talk with Alice Palmer. I know about how you lifted Jane's diary and photocopied one of the pages."

Patty stopped smiling. "Love to see you prove it."

"I don't have to prove it, because I don't care about it. All I want to know is how Jane died."

"She drowned."

"No, she didn't. When she went overboard, she slipped into scuba equipment, swam to the beach, and drove to Sharon's cabin."

"Really? That's far out."

"Yeah, but she died in the cabin. She burned to death. Do you know anything about that?"

"Nope."

"You don't seem very upset at the news."

"Because I don't believe you. Jane drowned."

"You are being held for involuntary manslaughter. There are witnesses who say you pushed Jane overboard. Would you believe me if I told you we will drop the charge if you answer a few questions?"

Patty showed renewed interest. "What are the questions?"

"Before we begin, how long have you been here at the station?"

"Since eleven this evening."

When they discovered the burned body in the cabin, his captain had felt it too much of a coincidence after the events on the boat, what with kids from Wilcox High being involved both times. Yet he'd had nothing tangible to connect the events. His sending a patrol car for Patty, after having released her only a few hours before, had seemed at first to be nothing but a formality.

"In between the time you were released this afternoon and the time you were brought in this evening, where were you?" he asked.

"Out."

"Out where? And with whom?"

"At the stores, hanging out by myself."

"Is there anyone who can verify your whereabouts shortly after sunset?" The cabin had apparently caught fire then.

"Nope."

"Why not?"

"I told you, I was out by myself."

"While you were out, did you swing by the hills, by any chance?"

"Not me. You were serious when you said Jane went up in smoke?"

"Yes."

She made a face. "How gross."

"Patty, I won't fool with you. I think we have a murder here. And since you were known to be a thorn in Jane's side, I strongly recommend you don't fool with me."

Anger entered her voice. "Is this how you drop my charge? By replacing it with a worse one?" She turned away. "I don't think I should talk to you anymore."

"If you didn't kill Jane, you should be anxious to talk to me."

"I didn't kill her!"

"Shh, not so loud. All right, you're innocent. I believe you. Where were you between your visits to the station?"

"Shopping. I love to shop."

"Did you buy anything?"

"Nope."

Fisher sighed to himself. He didn't have to worry about this girl breaking down and crying. "Do you know where Sharon is?"

"Have you tried her house?"

"She's not there. If you had to pick someone as a potential murderer of Jane, who would you choose?"

"That sounds like an incriminating question."

"Just answer it, please."

"Alice's dad."

"Come again?"

Patty leaned close, spoke confidentially. "I've watched that fat-ass since I was ten. He's my dentist. He's got deep sexual hang-ups, if you know what I mean. He's got something against the human body, thinks it's disgusting. He must look in the mirror too much. He probably heard what Jane wrote in her diary and wasted her before she could contaminate his darling daughter."

The idea sounded preposterous, yet there was something in it that made Fisher unwilling to dismiss it out of hand. "How would he have known where she was, even that she was still alive?" he asked.

"This summer, I got fitted for a diaphragm at the free clinic. When I went to Palmer's office the next week to have my teeth cleaned, he'd heard about it. He drills more than the teeth of the people who sit in his chair. He gets all the gossip. If Jane talked about her plan, I guarantee you, he heard about it."

According to Alice, Jane had explained her plan to Sharon in Dr. Palmer's office. Talk about co-incidence . . .

Have I been interrogating the wrong person?

Fisher got slowly to his feet. "One last question. Does Alice share her dad's sexual hang-ups?"

"I don't know. I suppose Kirk could have told you." Patty's nostrils suddenly flared. She had no doubt finally tied in what he had revealed about the hidden scuba equipment with Kirk's death. "Damn that Jane."

"That's not a nice thing to say about a dead girl."

Patty looked at him. "I just want to get out of here."

He found Officer Rick a few minutes later washing his face in the bathroom. "These late nights are really getting to me," the young man said, splashing cold water in his red eyes.

"You'll be going home soon," Fisher said, leaning against the white-tiled wall. "Heard anything else from our team at the cabin?"

Officer Rick reached for a paper towel. "They say if there's another body in the ashes, they're not going to find it without some sun."

"They've given up, then?"

"Yeah, think so."

"I forgot to ask this earlier. Did they say anything about a car parked outside the cabin?"

"No. There were no vehicles in the immediate vicinity."

"That's odd, isn't it?"

Rick wiped at his face. "I told you earlier, this whole damn thing is odd. Get any useful info out of the Palmer girl?"

Fisher nodded. "She had a lot to say. I'll tell you about it in the morning." He lifted himself off the wall. "Oh, did Dr. Hilt perform an autopsy on Kirk Donner?"

"What for? The kid drowned."

And when have I heard that one before?

"Do you think Hilt's still at the lab?" Fisher asked.

"Probably. Those coroners are all ghouls. They've got to be to stay in that line of work. He doesn't leave his lab all night."

"Do me one last favor before you leave. Tell Dr. Hilt to do a full autopsy on Kirk. Get permission from the parents. Tell the doctor I'm particularly curious to see if there was anything unusual in the boy's blood. If I'm not here, he can call me at home when he's done. I don't care what time it is."

"On to something?"

Fisher shook his head. "I'm clawing at thin air."

When he returned to Alice, the father was there. The two were preparing to leave. Dr. Palmer scowled when he saw him.

"You lied to me, young man," the dentist said. "You said you only needed a few minutes, and now look what time it is. My daughter is going home and going to bed this instant and I don't care what you say."

Alice stood docile by her father's side, a hand pressed to the side of her mouth, her eyes toward the floor.

"The situation turned out to be more complex than I had imagined," Fisher said.

"Now, I don't want any of your fancy excuses," Dr. Palmer said. "I've already filed a complaint with your captain. At least there's a man who respects a person's rights."

The irony of the situation did not escape Fisher. It had been the captain who had purposely distracted Dr. Palmer so that Alice could be questioned at length.

"Dr. Palmer, hasn't Jane Retton been an employee

of yours for some time?" Fisher asked. "And wasn't she also a close friend of your daughter's?"

The man was suspicious. "What's your point?"

"My point, sir, is that you don't appear to give a damn about what's happened to her."

The man's bulging neck turned a deep shade of red. He poked the air with his finger. "You stop right there! I always did the best I could for Jane, tried to show her the right way to behave. It's not my fault she got involved with the wrong kind of boys."

Fisher let his irritation show. "And what in heaven's name does her taste in boys have to do with her death?"

Dr. Palmer gave him an icy glare. "I believe, Lieutenant, you have overstepped your authority. I wouldn't be surprised if, when I speak to my daughter later, I discover you tried to take advantage of her."

"No, Father, he's been very polite," Alice said.

"Keep still, child," Dr. Palmer snapped. He ushered her toward the door. "We're leaving now. We're saying nothing more."

"We'll be calling you tomorrow," Fisher said as they were going out the door. "We need verification of both your whereabouts during the hour before and the hour after sunset on Saturday evening."

Dr. Palmer paused, glanced over his shoulder. "We were home alone together."

"Mrs. Palmer was away?"

"Mrs. Palmer has been away for the last ten years," Dr. Palmer said bitterly.

I don't blame her.

"Have a good night, Alice," Fisher said.

* * *

124

Fisher made a full oral report to the captain. When he finished, the captain asked him what had happened to teenagers whose biggest worries were what color lipstick to wear and who was taking them to the prom. Times have changed, Fisher replied. They both agreed they would have a busy day ahead of them tomorrow checking on the accuracy of Alice's statements.

But as Fisher left the station, the nagging feeling that tomorrow would be too late stayed with him. He attempted unsuccessfully to pinpoint the source of the disquiet. Dr. Palmer and Alice wouldn't be leaving town. Kirk and Jane could come to no greater harm. And Sharon would have to show up sooner or later. No, there was no reason he shouldn't go home, curl up in bed, and let the world turn without him for a few hours.

But Jane didn't walk to the cabin. What became of her car?

Fisher ended up on the road to the hills, the address of the Less's place tucked in his shirt pocket. The drive took him exactly thirty minutes. He arrived at the spot at a quarter after four.

Fisher had served as a medic in Vietnam. What was left of the cabin reminded him of a bunker he had been living in that had been hit by a VC rocket. It was a black scar on the hills. His associates had closed off the site with a red ribbon that wouldn't have discouraged a rabbit. Fisher parked and climbed out, his flashlight in hand

His stroll through the ashes did nothing to settle his mind. The fireplace had survived, the blackened plumbing, the posts that supported the rear of the house—little else. The association to the war had

come and wouldn't leave him. Seventeen-year-olds—
not really much younger than a lot of his buddies who
had died overseas.

*You couldn't have driven away from this. No one
could have.*

Fisher finally figured out what was haunting him.
Hope.

On the way down the hill, he drove far slower, his
search beam alternately scanning both sides of the
road. He had gone only a few hundred yards when he
caught a glint of metal in the bushes. He pulled on the
brake and got out.

It was a bicycle, a new Schwinn ten-speed. Fisher
glanced up the road; the incline immediately before
the cabin was extremely steep. A person familiar with
precisely how far there was left to go might have
parked the bike out of sight and walked the rest of the
way. Alice had mentioned something about Sharon
having lost her license.

Hilt used the skull, the teeth, to make a positive I.D.

Covering his hands with plastic gloves, Fisher lifted
the bike and stowed it in his trunk. He continued
down the road, continuing his search. Ten minutes
later he made a second discovery.

There were tire tracks in the soil beside the climbing
lane. For the third time, Fisher parked and stepped
outside with his flashlight. Two sets of tracks over-
lapped in places. The lighter tracks would be the
older. Apparently, the car had been parked facing
uphill. When it had been restarted, however, the
driver had backed up before turning around, rather
than simply going forward and turning. Fisher
crouched close to the dirt. There were footprints
beside the tracks pointing down the hill, several of

them rather deep. Whoever the driver had been, he or she had been pushing hard off the ground. . . .

Pushing!

Perhaps the car had been out of gas and it had been pushed down the hill to build up enough momentum to change direction, perhaps as a prelude to coasting all the way out of the hills. Coasting appeared feasible; the decline remained steady till the city limits. The more Fisher thought about it, the more convinced he became that his imaginary scenario was correct.

A bit of red caught his eye in the heel of the last footprint. He picked it up and laid it in his handkerchief, studying it under the full glare of the flashlight.

Hilt compared the teeth of the burned skull to dental X-rays.

Jane worked in her own dentist's office, and Palmer was also Sharon's dentist. She would have known where all the X-rays were stored, and how to switch two sets around.

Fisher was holding a piece of burned skin.

He jumped into his car and floored the accelerator.

CHAPTER XII

A NIGHTMARE.

It caught Jane Retton in the region between waking and sleep. Like many bad dreams, it came in darkness and had hidden within it a thing her heart sensed more than her eyes saw. From this thing emanated a scorching heat and a palpable intelligence that made her cringe in terror. It was aware. It had a purpose. It made evil plans. And it was so close it could almost touch her. The only way to escape it, she knew, was to hold her breath, to play dead. Then maybe it would pass her by and go on to another victim.

But how long can anyone hold their breath? Stuck underwater, a minute could be a long time. Boxed in a smoke-filled room, ten seconds might seem like an eternity. She had lived through both, gone through fire and ice, only to get trapped in this place with this monster. It wasn't fair. She would have to breathe soon. She could feel herself beginning to smother, her heart pounding harder and louder, so loud it seemed impossible the thing couldn't hear, impossible it wouldn't find her and then burn her with the slow, agonizing zeal of a fallen angel of death. . . .

"Angel," Jane gasped, sitting suddenly upright, drenched in sweat, blood throbbing in her head. The remainder of reality came back hard. She was hiding in Alice's dark bedroom closet. The air was stuffy and warm. From a rack overhead hung a thousand dresses she couldn't quite keep out of her face. The soles of her feet were burned to a crisp. And Sharon was no more. . . .

In the end, I did leave her.

She checked her watch: ten minutes to four. She had been in the closet several hours. She didn't care. She was prepared to wait forever.

What had awakened her? A car door slamming on the street outside? She listened for a minute, heard nothing. Wincing in pain, she realized it had probably been her injuries. She'd once read where a doctor had said nothing could cause more suffering than a serious burn. The guy had known what he was talking about.

Turning on a penlight, Jane examined the articles she had stolen from Dr. Palmer's clinic earlier in the night: rolls of bandage, a bottle of cocaine solution, and a flask of chloroform. The cocaine solution was almost gone; the container had been only a quarter full to start with. Dr. Palmer used a drop of it on a patient's gums prior to Novocain injections to dull the prick of the needle. Unwrapping her bloody bandages, Jane used a couple of ounces to recoat the soles of her feet. What she really needed was to take a painkiller internally; however, with what she was planning, she dared not risk it. She'd need all her wits. She'd been a fool to fall asleep. Alice could have entered the room and heard her breathing. But perhaps that's why she had dreamed of smothering. Even unconscious, she'd been trying to hold her breath.

Not for the first time today.

The cocaine solution worked, to a degree. She

supposed that without it she would be writhing in agony. She tried to concentrate on applying it while simultaneously trying not to look at how black and raw her feet had become since she'd fled the cabin. Her hands were shaking. If she'd had anything left in her stomach, she probably would have thrown up.

She did the next worst thing. Her nerves were shot.

It started off as a violent cough. The smoke had damaged her lungs; breathing was irritating. But then her choking turned to uncontrollable sobs. She had left Sharon on the floor of the bathroom with fire crawling toward her hair. A minute more and she would've had to watch her burn. Yet even having been spared the view of the final destruction of Sharon's life, Jane couldn't get the picture out of her mind. Her imagination was worse than reality, and this reality had come straight out of hell. Her only consolation was that Jane Retton still lived, and that Sharon's— and Kirk's—death could be avenged.

Revenge? Isn't that what killed them in the first place?

She tried to push the thought away and couldn't. She had not fired the gun. She had not thrown the bottle of gasoline. Nevertheless, she couldn't escape the fact that she had set everything in motion with her need to get even. Had she been a little less worried about her goddamn reputation, she would still have a boyfriend, and a best friend.

Why didn't I look at her, even for a second, before I brained her? Why did I care who knew I was horny, when everyone is horny?

She cried a long time, but the tears washed away neither her pain nor her hate. True, she accepted her share of the blame, but only her share. The other one was going to pay, too. She'd salvaged something else from the inferno besides her damaged body. The gun she'd found beneath the pillow now rested between her legs.

The garage door began to open. Jane set aside the cocaine solution and uncorked the flask of chloroform. Winding several feet of fresh gauze into a fist-sized ball, she found she was trembling in anticipation.

She could hear the automated garage door shutting, car doors opening and closing, voices entering the kitchen. The house was long, but words travel far when being overheard by an attentive listener sitting in a quiet place. Jane cracked the closet door slightly. A private father-daughter chat. How interesting. . . .

"I don't care how tired you are in the morning," Dr. Palmer said. "You're going to church. People will talk if you don't. They're going to talk, anyway. From now on, I'm having more say about who you associate with. Take that Sharon, for instance. She was a friend of Jane's. She must have been influenced by her. And now you tell me the police think she's run off somewhere? Friends like that, I don't want to see them around here. Are you listening to me?"

"Yes, Father. I don't think I'll be seeing Sharon that much from now on."

Jane checked the revolver's chamber. Six bullets.

"And another thing, you should never have dragged me down to the police station tonight. You should have let sleeping dogs lie. The police don't have the caliber of men they used to. Nowadays they are only interested in one thing, finding someone to pin the blame on. They care nothing about right or wrong. Take that insolent detective, for example. He was bad.

You couldn't see it, but I could tell right away he thought you were responsible for Kirk and Jane drowning."

"Father, Jane didn't drown. She got caught in a fire in the hills."

"That's my point! What was she doing up in the hills? Here we ruin our trip searching for her in the water and she's off somewhere, laughing her head off. How can I feel sympathy for someone like that? I should have told that smart-mouthed cop as much. He had a nerve implying I'm not upset by what has happened. Of course I'm upset. For the love of God, they were only children. It must be terrible for their parents. But it just irritates me no end that Sharon was right there with us on the boat and knew exactly where Jane was and didn't say a word. I never want to catch that girl in this house again, you hear me?"

"All right."

Damn.

Suddenly Dr. Palmer drastically lowered his voice, and even after opening the closet door the whole way, Jane could hear him only in patches.

"You were there when . . . that detective asked . . . we discussed on the way to the station . . . I want you to tell me . . . explain that you went . . . by yourself?"

Alice's answer was softer still, almost unintelligible. Jane caught the word *movie*, nothing else.

Dr. Palmer continued: "But what if someone remembers you . . . could tell the police . . . there would be . . . in your story . . . get in trouble."

Jane decided this portion of the conversation was too crucial to be missed. She went so far as to lean outside the closet. Unfortunately, she caught only a few words of Alice's reply: "Honestly, you don't have to worry."

Then Dr. Palmer's mood underwent one of its famous shifts, and his volume increased along with his warmth. "I should be congratulating you on your sense of duty. You're a brave girl. You didn't have to subject yourself to all that torment."

Alice's voice also returned to a normal level. "I wanted to help. Oh, Father, I'll miss them."

Gimme a break.

He must have hugged her. "Don't cry, Alice. The Lord is forgiving. Tomorrow we'll say a prayer for them both. Now you go to bed. You've had a long day."

"Good night. Thanks so much for your help."

"Sweet dreams, angel."

Jane shut the closet door. She opened the flask of chloroform, carefully covered the neck with the wad of gauze, and inverted the flask. One small whiff of the anesthetic made her head spin slightly. Replacing the cork, she turned off her penlight and rose to her knees. Jane had slept over before. Alice always used the closet for one reason or another before going to bed.

Come to me, dear friend.

Alice entered the bathroom first. There it seemed she brushed and flossed her teeth for hours. Had to keep up that bright smile for the funeral pictures, Jane thought bitterly. Next Alice sat on the bed, where she was probably removing her shoes, undressing. This, too, took an unusually long time, and Jane listened closely, expecting to hear perhaps a few tears of guilt. But if Alice wept, she did so in the privacy of her soul.

Finally Alice stood and walked toward the closet.

Jane silently drew in a breath, remembering the fire poker, the head pushing through the door at the cabin. At least this time she knew who the enemy was.

The door slid open. Alice reached inside and touched a purple nightgown. Crouched on Alice's left, Jane suddenly stood and grabbed Alice's arm, yanking her into the closet and simultaneously turning her around. Caught off balance, Alice toppled backward, a faint gasp escaping her lips. Jane supported her long enough to press the chloroform-soaked bandage over her nose and mouth.

"Breathe, angel," Jane hissed in her ear. "While you still can."

Alice's bulging eyes rolled back to see who was attacking her. For an instant, she struggled. She even tried to scream, but in the attempt, she breathed. Then her eyes rolled all the way back in her head and her body went limp in Jane's arms.

Sweet dreams, bitch.

While Jane had been raiding Dr. Palmer's pharmaceutical cabinet and rearranging his patient records, she had also had the foresight to steal the extra set of keys he kept in his desk. They had given her easy access to the house. There were passes to all sorts of places on Dr. Palmer's key chain. If she had wanted to, and had had the strength, she could have unlocked his garage, stowed Alice in the trunk of the car, started the car, driven down to the marina, loaded Alice on board his boat, started the boat, and sailed out to sea where no one would have been able to question a single aspect of her interrogation methods.

Unfortunately, she did not have the strength, or the pain threshold, to carry out such a scheme. The

Palmers had a very small guest house on the far side of their swimming pool. The windows had been boarded up—it was just like him to board something up that rarely saw use—and a good fifty yards lay between it and Dr. Palmer's bedroom. The long silver key in the center of the chain fit its lock. The guest house was where Alice would talk.

Walking hurt. Having to drag a body didn't help. Before she could even reach the bedroom door with Alice, Jane had to stop, undo the bandages on her feet, and pour the remainder of the numbing solution over her meaty flesh. The stuff appeared to be losing potency. She was using far more with less effect. Or perhaps walking was worsening her condition. She wondered briefly if the nerves on the soles of her feet had been permanently destroyed, if she would ever walk normally again.

No matter what happens with Alice, I'll pay for this.

One thing favored her. Cracking the door to Alice's bedroom, she heard loud snores coming from the other side of the house. A few minutes in bed and he was out cold; the sleep of an innocent man? It made her wonder. Somehow, somewhere, that guy must have had a hand in all this madness.

He's probably going to welch on paying me last week's salary.

The concrete around the pool gave Jane the most trouble. Each time she put pressure on her feet, yanking Alice forward, it felt as if another inch of her skin had been rubbed off. She'd wound fresh gauze over the old bandage after applying the last of the cocaine solution, but the red was already showing through.

The guest house door had to be smacked open.

Panting heavily, Jane bent over and dragged Alice the last few feet. Then she closed the door and collapsed on the floor. The only light was paper-thin slices of white from the late moon shining through cracks between the boards Dr. Palmer had nailed over the windows.

Jane was not an expert on drug dosages. She didn't know when Alice's anesthesia would wear off.

I'll poke her every few minutes.

Alice did not keep her waiting long. Before Jane had fully caught her breath, Alice moaned softly, stretching like someone coming out of a lengthy sleep, then opened her eyes and stared at the ceiling. Jane pulled the revolver from her belt.

"If you cry out," she said calmly, "I'll blow your goddamn head off."

Alice sat up, dazed. "What— Jane?"

"I'm glad you remember me." She held the barrel in a narrow shaft of moonlight, giving Alice a good look at it. "I was afraid maybe you had forgotten your friends."

Alice stifled a yawn, stared at her closely. "I'm dreaming," she said finally.

"No."

"But you're dead. The fire got you."

Jane did not answer immediately, slowly undoing the bandages on her right foot with her free hand. "You forgot when you cornered me in the cabin that I had scuba equipment. And even with all the flames, the plumbing took awhile to fail. You don't see the connection? I suppose I can't blame you. It took me until the last minute to realize that with a full wet suit, a face mask, water, and an air tank, I had a way out."

"Wnat are you talking about?"

"You can trap a lot of water under a wet suit. It makes excellent insulation, that is, until the suit starts to melt. But when the thing is soaked on the outside as well as on the inside, you have awhile—five, maybe six seconds. Long enough to run downstairs and out the front door. I'm glad you finally decided to leave, Alice. I was a bit worried you were going to shoot me, and after I had gone to so much trouble to save myself. But I suppose you figured there was no point in staying after you shot at me up in the bedroom. That movie you'd told your father about must have been ready to get out."

Alice shook her head. "What movie? You're making no sense."

"Are you wondering about my feet? The suit doesn't cover them, I know. I can understand how you might be confused. You see, I just grabbed whatever shoes were handy. Even soaked, they didn't protect me very well." Jane pulled away the last of her bandage, showing the penlight over her toes. Seeing, and smelling, the ruined flesh, Alice let out a gasp. Jane added, "Not very pretty, are they?"

"But the police identified your body."

"I went to the clinic. I have a key, remember? I switched Sharon's X-rays with mine." She had skipped the parts about coasting out of the hills on an empty tank, bumming gas from the station at the bottom of the last hill after flashing her feet and moaning that she was on her way to the hospital—the fellow had wanted to drive her—and her stop at home to change out of the melted wet suit, but she supposed now was not the time to go into every blessed detail.

"Sharon's dead?"

"Yes."

Alice sighed softly. "I'm glad you made it. It's a miracle."

"I don't believe in miracles, angel."

Alice paused, nodded toward the gun. "What's that for?"

"It's used for killing people."

Alice raised an eyebrow. "Why did you say when *I* cornered you in the cabin? I wasn't at the cabin."

"I suppose the squirrels threw that Molotov cocktail at me?"

"The what?"

"That's what it's called when you fill a bottle with gasoline, jam a rag in the top, and set it on fire." Jane leaned closer, raising the revolver level with Alice's big eyes. "I want you to tell me the whole story, from beginning to end. Then I'll decide whether I'm going to blow your brains out."

"You're mad."

Jane chuckled softly. "No, I'm dead. You said it yourself." She shook the gun. "Talk."

"About what?"

"You can start with how you killed Kirk."

"Kirk drowned, searching for you."

"You lie. If you'd tied his hands behind his back and dumped him a mile off shore, he wouldn't have drowned."

"What makes you think I know anything about this?"

"Sharon had instructions not to tell you about my plan until after I went in the water. Since Kirk just happened to die right after that, and since you've hated Kirk for the last six months, I must assume you knew about my plan beforehand and that you used the opportunity to kill Kirk."

"That's quite an assumption," Alice said. The tone of her voice disturbed Jane. It was flat, indifferent, as if she was going through something for the second time and finding it boring. She did not appear frightened.

"It's what happened!"

"Really? And how did I kill Kirk in front of all those people without anyone seeing me?"

"I'm not sure. But no one knew I was at the cabin except you and Sharon. Or are you going to deny Sharon told you about my plan at all?"

"She told me."

"When?"

"Later, when we were back on shore."

"I think you're lying. Sharon never could keep secrets. I think she told you earlier."

"If Sharon had such a big mouth, how do you know she didn't tell a lot of people?"

"She wouldn't have done that. She might have talked too much, but she was never disloyal." Jane pulled her exposed foot back, pain pulsing up both her legs. Alice had an answer for everything. This was not going as she had planned. "But none of this matters. You made a mistake at the beginning. I've been remembering how you went into my bedroom to get Sharon, how, like Sharon, you were gone awhile. And then, later, you showed up at my homeroom. You'd never done that before. Sure, you had some excuse, but it was pretty thin. You motioned me into the hallway, and then told me to wait outside while you went in and talked to Patty. Quite a coincidence, don't you think, that Patty should come up with my diary not long after?"

"Sharon came by your homeroom, too."

"Sharon's dead. In my book, that makes her innocent."

Alice remained unimpressed. "Anything else?"

"Dammit, I know it was you up at the cabin! And I know you killed Kirk! And I know why you killed him." Then she made a stab in the dark. No, not totally in the dark. Perhaps her intuition guided her, maybe her subconscious. During the hours she had waited in Alice's closet, she had rolled the question over and over in her thoughts: *why?* No clear answer had presented itself, but the unusual manner in which Alice had dumped Kirk had gnawed at her. Kirk *had* to be the connection; Alice had made him her first target, and they'd both had him as a boyfriend. Filling her voice with scorn, Jane said, "He told me what he did to you."

She'd hit a vital spot. Alice lifted her head. "What did he tell you?" she whispered.

"He told me everything. At first, I thought he must have been kidding. Who would have thought that about you?"

Alice began to tremble. "Kirk was a fool."

"You were the fool!"

"What did he tell you?"

Jane giggled, moving blindly. "He told me how he *ruined* you."

Alice slapped her across the face. For a moment Jane was so startled—she did have a gun, after all—that she didn't know what to do. Then she slapped her back. She put a lot of anger into the blow, knocking Alice over. She didn't really mind, however, when Alice sprang right back and tried to tackle her. The frustration had been building; Jane was ready and willing to pull Alice's hair out. Tossing aside the gun, not minding how much noise they were making, she went at it.

But their wrestling match didn't last long. They didn't even finish round one. Alice dived into her head first, they completed a couple of rolls across the floor, scratching at each other, and then Alice quit. As she straddled Alice, Jane got the surprise of her life when Alice started bawling.

"He did ruin me," Alice moaned. "He wrecked my life."

Jane moved carefully aside and sat down on the floor. "How?"

Although Alice indirectly answered the question, Jane doubted she had heard it. She appeared to speak to another, to someone not present. Or perhaps she spoke to herself. There was agony in her voice. "He gave it to me. He needed to get rid of it. He didn't care about me. He didn't care what my father would say."

"What did he give you, Alice?"

Alice sat up, moving as if in a dream, the slivers of moonlight filtering through her lustrous black hair. It was an absurd thought to have under the circumstances, but Jane couldn't help marveling at how beautiful she was. "You know, Jane," she mumbled. "Everyone knows."

"Tell me."

Alice hung her head at a weird angle, as if she were a marionette having trouble with a string. It seemed unlikely, but Jane's made up comment about what Kirk had said had totally devastated Alice. "I don't care about your gun, Jane. You shouldn't have cared about mine. Everybody knows about us. They've read your diary. And they've just got to look at me. We would be better off dead."

"What do they know about you?"

As Alice rolled her head to the other side, a moon-beam cut across her face. It must have been the light; there wasn't a trace of color in her skin. "I shouldn't have bothered," she muttered, staring off into the distance. "I should have just quit. I should have dumped him and not bothered with you." She smiled to herself, a sad smile. "But I was afraid you would figure me out and turn me in." She shrugged. "Where's your gun, Jane? I'm not afraid. Come on, shoot me. Go ahead, I won't tell anybody."

"I'm not going to hurt you." The words had a power all their own. Jane's fury, her overwhelming desire for vengeance—they didn't vanish, but they were set aside, making room for something stronger—curiosity. "I want to understand."

Alice sighed, then stood up. "You were always a big one for stories, Jane. You like to read other people's lies. What do you want to hear?" She stood above her, looking down. "I'll tell you anything you want to hear."

"Did you give Patty the diary?"

"In a way. When I went into your homeroom, I set it on top of your book bag, open to your last entry. I thought Patty would see it, and take it." Alice turned away. "She didn't disappoint me."

"How did Kirk die?"

Alice stepped to the door, removed something small and round from a nearby shelf. Jane supposed she should stand, see what Alice was doing. Yet Alice's whole persona had changed with her admission—if it could be called that; it had explained nothing—that Kirk had ruined her life. She didn't seem in the least threatening. She, in fact, appeared totally crushed.

What could he possibly have done?

Jane hadn't replaced the bandage on her right foot; the thought of putting her bloody flesh directly on the hard floor was not appealing. No, she would stay, for the moment, where she was.

"He kept diving deeper and deeper," Alice said. "He was worried about you. He followed me way down, near the bottom. I offered him a lungful from my right tank." She clicked the object onto some sort of link on the door. Jane could see it now—a padlock. Alice added, "He didn't stand a chance. No one does in this world."

"What do you mean, your right tank? You always use a single tank."

Alice stepped away from the door, heading toward the rear of the room. Jane had misplaced her penlight; following Alice was difficult. From what she could see, it appeared that Dr. Palmer used the guest house for storage. Perhaps that was the reason he kept it all locked up. Boxes lined the walls. Alice touched a cylindrical object. Jane heard metal clink against metal; there were a number of air tanks standing in a row.

"This was my right tank," Alice said. "I filled it special for our trip, after Sharon told me what you were up to."

"When did Sharon tell you?"

"Does it matter? Before you wanted her to. She was concerned you might hurt yourself. She wanted my opinion. I told her there was nothing to worry about."

"What's in that tank?"

"Nitrous oxide, laughing gas."

"You went diving carrying gas?"

Alice had her back to Jane, bent over the equipment. "I had two tanks. One for me, one for Kirk. One had fresh air, the other had gas. I had two mouth-pieces. Nobody noticed. I used my father's old anesthesia supplies. It was easy to transfer the gas to an empty scuba tank. I just had to connect them. The pressure did the rest." She coughed thickly. "I knocked Kirk out forty feet beneath the surface."

A wave of nausea and grief swept over Jane. Her beautiful boyfriend—put into a death sleep as if he were a pet being put out of its misery. Her vision blurred. She must be crying again.

And you were trying to save me.

"But why, Alice?" She wept. "Why?"

Alice nodded, turning to face her. "You're crying. I cried a lot. I'm tired of it. You must be, too."

A faint sound caught Jane's ears. At first it appeared to be coming from far off, a wind rising over the ocean, perhaps. She shook her head. No, it was steady, constant. "What is that?"

"I'm not crazy, Jane. A crazy person doesn't know what she's doing. It's just that lately I've been so upset. I'd see you and Kirk together, holding hands, smiling, kissing." She winced. "And then it came back and wouldn't go away, and I—" A shudder went through her. "My father says that if we ask, we will be forgiven. Maybe we should ask together, Jane, right now."

"Your father! That jerk knew all about this."

"No." Alice gave a twisted smile. "When I was at the cabin, he thought I was watching a Disney film."

Jane noticed a sweet odor, and the sound she'd heard a moment ago finally registered in her mind as a steady hiss. "What's that noise?" she asked again.

"Gas."

"What?" Jane jumped up and promptly fell straight over, letting out a cry. Without the bandage, walking wasn't simply painful, it was impossible. "You opened the valve on the tank!"

Alice wheezed. "Yeah."

Jane scrambled to her knees. "But the gas will knock us out! Close it!"

Alice turned and picked up the tank, rocking on her feet. The gas, regrettably, hadn't gone too deep into her blood. She had strength enough to heave the tank into the air. It disappeared behind a stack of blankets stored on a corner loft, out of reach without a ladder. Alice coughed. "It'll take just a minute to empty."

Yet it had already begun to spread. Dizziness hit Jane, tilting the room at a peculiar angle. On her hands and knees, holding on to the floor, she crawled to the door, reached up and tugged on the lock. "Where's the key to this thing?" she demanded.

Alice stumbled toward her, using the wall for support. "I can't remember," she said groggily. "But I know where the matches are."

"The matches?"

"I'm going to light a candle."

"No! You'll blow us up!"

Alice pulled open a cabinet, banging her head on its door. "I love candles. I love red ones."

Jane didn't know what to do. She assumed the gas would explode, but all of a sudden she couldn't think straight. There had to be another way out, a back door. Every place had a back exit, except that crazy cabin in the hills. As she scrutinized the rear of the house, however, all she could make out was a fuzzy cloud of nothing. That nothing had to be the cloud of gas, she decided. Yeah, it wouldn't be smart to go that way. That gas was bad stuff. It dried up the old brain cells.

It's already in your brain, idiot!

Struggling against the effects of the anesthesic, the sound of the escaping gas hissing in her ears, the sweet taste of it in her mouth, Jane pushed herself away from the door and picked up the discarded revolver. Pointing the barrel at the lock, she pulled the trigger. Nothing happened.

You hid it under your wet suit while running out of the cabin. There must be water in the chamber. But you're lucky it didn't work. The spark might have triggered the gas.

Jane nodded to herself at the reasonableness of the explanation. It was that way now; there were voices in her head telling her things and there were mushy thoughts trying to understand the voices. A pity they were both talking at the same time. She didn't know which one to listen to. But one thing for sure, she didn't want any more fires. She groped her way toward Alice. By the time she reached her, Alice had toppled to the floor. In her hands, however, she held a box of matches and a red Christmas candle.

"In Girl Scouts," Alice said, pressing the tip of a match to the rough side of the box. "I learned how to start a fire without a stove."

"Stop that," Jane cried feebly, knocking the match from her hands.

Alice looked at her with something akin to impatience, picked the match back up. "You hurt my hand, Jane."

Jane rubbed her eyes, blinking. There was nothing wrong with Alice's hands. It was her own feet that had been hurt. "I did not," she said. "Don't light the match."

"I will if I want to. You can't tell me what to do."

Jane reached over—it was a long way over—and took the match away from Alice. Now what was she supposed to do with it? She couldn't remember. "You're stupid," she said. "You killed Kirk, and he was a nice guy."

Alice got excited. "He wasn't nice! He was bad!"

"No, he wasn't. He liked me. I liked him."

This is not the time for conversation. You have to get outside, into the fresh air.

But getting up seemed such a bother. Her eyelids felt as if they were holding up the world. She closed them briefly, reopened them with an effort. Alice was shaking her head impatiently.

"You don't know anything. You're the one who's stupid. If I told what he did to me, you'd say you didn't like him either. That's what you would say."

Jane strained to hold on to her mind. This aspect of the discussion was important. She was pretty sure it was. "What did he do to you?"

Alice began to cry. "My father told me boys will give you things. I should have listened to my father."

Jane frowned, trying to put it all together. The only thing Kirk had owned was his truck, and he had never given that to Alice. "Did he give it to you for Christmas?"

Alice cried harder, taking another match out of her tiny cardboard box. "I don't know when! He just gave it to me! He had to get rid of it so he could get another girlfriend!"

"Did he wrap it up for you?"

"No! You don't wrap up a disease!"

Jane gasped. The shock of the revelation cleared her mind somewhat. This was it right here, the absolute unadulterated truth behind all truths. "Oh, my. You two had *sex*. Oh, boy."

Alice literally screamed at her. "No, we didn't! All he did was give me a kiss! A bad kiss!" She pointed to the sores on her lips. "See these? He gave me these!" Her face fell. "And I can't get rid of them."

"But they're just cold sores. Who cares?"

"Just cold sores! They're *herpes* sores! I've got a *venereal* disease!" She moaned pitifully. "No one will ever kiss me again. I'll have to keep them for the rest of my life."

Jane started laughing. She couldn't help herself. Even with Alice weeping her heart out beside her, she couldn't stop. "You dumb broad. Don't you know anything? Your dad's a dentist, for God's sake. You should know all about viruses."

Alice yawned loudly. The yawning combined with her crying made her sound like a seriously ill panda bear. "I know it's a virus. But it's different. Only bad boys can give it to you."

Jane continued to cackle like a hyena. "No one gives you a disease to get rid of it! Oh, you're too much! Fatty father has really messed up your head. That's what you get for pretending to be an angel."

Alice was indignant. "Then why do they give it to you if they're not trying to get rid of it?"

"It's a virus. Chicken pox, cold sores—it doesn't make any difference. They're just things you can catch." She started to cough. "They're not gifts."

"How come you didn't catch it from him, then, smarty pants?"

"I don't know, maybe I did," Jane gasped. This party was getting too wild. She was totally wasted. She should probably go home.

"Really? And you don't care?"

"Right now, I don't care if I care." Jane tried to get up. The floor flowed beneath her as if it were made of thawing ice. "Let's get out of here."

Alice pouted. "No." She took the match in her hand and attempted to strike it. She missed the box by a couple of inches. "I want to die."

Jane couldn't get her knees to bend forward. They wanted to go to the sides, in opposite directions. She collapsed backward into Alice. Miss Angel continued to try to light the candle. "Hey, I told you not to do that," Jane said.

"Why not? Let's die and put yourself out of my misery." Alice's aim improved. A whiff of smoke came from the match this time. Jane tried to stick out her hands and stop Alice, but she couldn't find her hands. She checked to see if they were still attached to the ends of her arms and couldn't find those either. That gas—there should be a law against it. Poor kids get hooked and they forget where their parts are.

"If you want to die, you go ahead and die," Jane mumbled. "But count me out. I've died twice today and that was twice too many times."

Alice ignored her, gathering together thirty matches in her three hundred fingers and pressing them securely to the dark sandpaper strips on the sides of all thirty of her cute little matchboxes. In that instant, a ray of clarity pierced Jane's cloudy mind. It brought fear, nothing more, nothing that could help. The situation was beyond her physical control. She couldn't even turn her head.

"He was a lousy kisser, anyway," Alice said as she went to strike the matches for what was sure to be the last time.

I thought he was fantastic.

The door burst open. A big man rushed in. He had to be ten feet tall. He waved his hands at the air. "Gas!" he cried. "You girls, get out of here!"

Alice dropped her matches. There were thousands of them now. They took years to reach the floor. Jane wondered who the man might be. He didn't look much like Kirk, but then, now that Kirk was an angel, he might look like Alice's brother. Only Alice didn't have a brother. Jane felt totally mixed up. Her moment of clarity had expired. But she was happy that there wouldn't be another fire and that the man was picking her up. His arms slid around her body and she floated in the direction of the door. The guest house fell behind. The moon shone in her eyes. And the outside air tasted wonderful. She drank it up in big hungry gulps.

"You rest here," the man said, putting her down beside the pool. "I'll get Alice."

"Don't kiss her," Jane said.

While she waited, she stretched her sore feet into the water, sending moonlit ripples careening toward the diving board. Watching them rebound and slowly return and overlap, Jane wondered if there was a symbolic significance to everything that had happened to her in the last couple of days. Probably not, she decided; her luck must have just taken a rotten turn.

A police siren started in the distance and grew louder and louder, snapping to a halt on the other side of the house. Jane heard voices, lots of footsteps.

The man reappeared with Alice and laid her on the grass near the pool heater. She seemed to be unconscious. Leaving Alice, the man walked back toward her. Following his legs from her ground-level perspective, Jane decided he couldn't be ten feet tall, after all.

If I think I'm waking up, I must be waking up.

The man knelt by her side. He had a charming face. She wondered if he was important. She hoped he was. She could write about him in her diary, how he had swooped through the flames to rescue her from the evil dragon queen.

"Are you okay, Jane?"

He knew her name. God bless him. "My feet hurt."

He pulled her legs from the water and studied her burns, his face darkening. "I'm taking you to the hospital."

"All right."

He picked her up again, and she cuddled into his chest. It had been awhile since she'd had an opportunity to relax. A shame Dr. Palmer's irritating voice had to ruin things.

"What are you doing here?" The dentist demanded, striding along the rim of the pool, dressed in Snoopy pajamas. He glanced in the direction of Alice. "What have you done to my daughter? Is that Jane you're carrying? You said she was dead. I knew it! This has all been a hoax. I want your badge number, Lieutenant. I'm going to report—"

The man threw a sharp elbow, catching Dr. Palmer square on the chest, sending him toppling into the pool. Jane felt the spray from the splash and heard a gurgling sound, but she didn't turn to watch the walrus struggle to stay afloat. She simply wasn't interested. Maintaining his calm pace, the man continued toward the side of the house, in the direction of the street.

"He can't swim," she muttered.

"Doesn't surprise me," the man said.

Several police appeared on the scene. The man directed them toward the pool with a nod of his head. One of the officers—he looked rather young—stopped to speak to the man.

"I heard your call on the radio," he said.

"I thought you'd be home in bed by now, Rick."

"I was, couldn't sleep. Who's the girl?"

The man laughed softly. "Remember how Jane Retton drowned in the ocean and then burned to death in the hills?"

The young officer took a step back. "This ain't her, is it? Oh, man, I tell you, this gives me the creeps. How does she keep coming back to life?"

"I'll explain it all later, Rick." The man stepped by. "I have to go. She has to see a doctor."

The officer shook his head. "Take my advice, pal, take her to a witch doctor."

As the man opened the door to his car and bent to place her on the front seat, a sudden rush of jumbled emotion went through Jane. Most of the feelings were dark, tied in the knots of personal loss. Yet from deep inside came an unlooked-for spark, something bright—maybe hope, possibly gratitude. She hugged the man's neck, afraid to let go. "Who are you?" she asked.

He smiled. "A friend."

"But I don't know you."

He set her in the car, brushed the hair from her eyes. "But I know you, Jane. I've been up the whole night thinking about you."

ABOUT THE AUTHOR

CHRISTOPHER PIKE was born in Brooklyn, New York, but grew up in Los Angeles, where he lives to this day. Prior to becoming a writer, he worked in a factory, painted houses and programmed computers. His hobbies include astronomy, meditating, running, playing with his nieces and nephews, and making sure his books are prominently displayed in local bookstores. He is the author of *Last Act, Spellbound, Gimme a Kiss* and *Final Friends I, II* and *III*, all available from Pocket Books. *Slumber Party, Weekend, Chain Letter, The Tachyon Web*, and *Sati*—an adult novel about a very unusual lady—are also by Mr. Pike.